private
LIES

private
LIES

TRUE STORIES FROM MY LIFE AS A
PRIVATE INVESTIGATOR

ALISON MARSH

First published in the UK in 2025 by Blink Publishing
An imprint of Bonnier Books UK
5th Floor, HYLO, 105 Bunhill Row,
London, EC1Y 8LZ

A CIP catalogue record for this book is available from the British Library.

Hardback ISBN: 9781789468403

Also available as an ebook and an audiobook

1 3 5 7 9 10 8 6 4 2

Design and Typeset by Envy Design Ltd
Printed and bound in Great Britain by Clays Ltd, Elcograf S.p.A.

The authorised representative in the EEA is
Bonnier Books UK (Ireland) Limited.
Registered office address: Floor 3, Block 3, Miesian Plaza,
Dublin 2, D02 Y754, Ireland
compliance@bonnierbooks.ie

www.bonnierbooks.co.uk

To my darling dad.
I hope that I have made you proud.
Love you always.
♡

CONTENTS

CHAPTER 1

Becoming Miss AM

'Please, can you help me?' are words you'll hear in any profession. From needing assistance in a shop to speaking to a doctor and everything in between. Sometimes asking for help is rather insignificant, but sometimes it can be the question to prevent heartbreak, financial ruin, or even physical danger. Asking a private investigator for help seems different. It's big. And it's a question I take very seriously. The people who come to me are desperate; they've exhausted all other avenues and they just need answers, even when those answers are unpalatable.

Often, when I mention that I am a private investigator, the other party thinks of a cliché that you'd see on TV or in a film – a mysterious man wearing a trilby hat and beige trench coat and carrying binoculars; or else

James Bond-esque secret agents, replete with codenames and fancy gadgets. I'm sorry to say this is – mostly – unrealistic. Before I discovered this career for myself, I'd probably have had the same film-noir expectations. Any misconceptions I had of shady fellows tucked down an alleyway was banished as I learned more about the ethics and standards that any self-respecting PI is bound by. There's a certain element of playing a part involved, but a personal connection with the people I serve performs a vital role in my ability to help. Results are important, but so is being able to look at myself in the mirror and stand by my actions.

If I had a pound for every time someone compared my job to Sherlock Holmes/James Bond/other clichéd spy, I'd be laughing all the way to the bank. But while I can't confirm or deny the existence of these archetypes in real life, I can say without a doubt that, with my red hair, chunky glasses and bold attire, I do not fit the bill. You won't see me in a deerstalker hat, puffing on a pipe, nor will you catch me chasing down the bad guy in unrealistically high boots and tight jeans. In fact, you won't catch me doing anything in tight jeans other than saying to myself, 'Who picked these bloody tight jeans!?'

For me, 'chasing down the bad guy' means something rather different. It's metaphorical; the Big Bad isn't (necessarily) an individual; it's lies, deception, fraud, heartache, loss, jealousy and suffering.

But that doesn't mean the career I've built over the

past several years isn't exciting. Stereotypes and jokes aside, my journey to becoming a private investigator has been utterly thrilling. From cheating spouses and stolen money, to mistrust and misunderstandings, there's never a dull day at the office for a PI.

If you were to ask me to summarise my profession in one word, I would say 'immeasurable'. The results I find for people can have a profound impact on their lives; it's much, much more than just digging up dirt. Private investigation is more vast, delicate, detailed and critical than that. It's more than idle gossip, and it's even more than knowing what to look for and where. It's my duty to peel back all of the layers and to keep going until I find the truth, and help guide my clients through the consequences of those findings.

A large, and arguably the most important, part of my job is dealing with, and helping other people deal with, the harsh facts of human nature. People lie, people deceive, people steal, and people cheat. Understanding the complexities of human behaviour and relationships is vital when trying to solve a case. Looking at the picture as a whole, rather than just the situation, is a crucial skill. When trying to prove or disprove someone's allegations, I have to look into the mind of the key parties and figure out the why, not just the what.

Every case requires a unique touch and draws on a variety of skills. No two cases are the same, ever. The only thing that remains the same throughout is my dedication to helping my client and getting to the bottom of the matter.

Usually, a career change is a calculated effort; one I never anticipated making. I wouldn't have expected at the age of fifty, after spending most of my life working as a carer in various capacities, to leave a job I cherished deeply for something new. I definitely wouldn't have expected to make the leap from care work to private investigation. The roles are worlds apart but, surprisingly, require a lot of overlapping skills – a kind ear and a strong constitution, to name just two. When I look back on the days before Miss AM, I find myself wondering why it took me so long to discover this version of myself, but a series of unexpected life-changing events turned my world upside down and led me down this path.

Everything that made me who I am and everything I thought I knew changed with the death of my father. All death is unexpected, really, and you might think that, with me in my fifties and he an impressive ninety-eight, I shouldn't have been quite so blindsided by his passing, but truly I was completely thunderstruck when it happened. I know losing a parent is one of those heartbreaking events that almost everyone experiences, but this drastic shift fundamentally changed me for ever.

My parents divorced when I was seven, leaving my dad to raise me alone. I only saw my mother for about six weeks out of the year and we never really had much of a bond. My brother and sister were much older, well into their adulthoods, and had their own lives when my parents split, so it wasn't much of an upheaval for them. It was just the two of us – me and my dad – navigating this new life. During that time, I never felt less than, or that I was missing something; it was all I knew and that was enough for me.

My dad was born in 1915 and was fifty-two when I was born. I can't imagine being fifty-two and starting over with a new child, yet my dad excelled at it. But as I write this, I realise that I was about the same age when I started this journey, and the thought makes me smile – we're even more alike than I'd realised. There was a vast generational gap between when my dad was brought up and when I was – even more so than between when I raised my daughter and now, when she's raising hers. He was skilled at blending the authoritarian way he was brought up with a gentler touch that a young pre-teen girl needed.

He was a skilled carpenter and made a lot of my toys by hand, from a small doll's house to a summer house that as a child I loved to play in. I spent a lot of my grouchy teenage years in there too; I think he had the foresight to create a space for me to escape during that time and I think he was more glad of it than I was. He made me a swing, which we would spend hours playing on during the warm summers, and a kite that had us both running up and down the steep hills near our home most days. I was a bossy little madam – still am, to be fair – but he often indulged me, knowing the line between treating me and not spoiling me. I remember chewing his ear off for weeks about buying a paddling pool for the upcoming summer months. I had a long list of jobs I had to achieve for him to 'see what he could do'. By the time the school holidays came, there was a wooden-framed pool waiting for me in the garden.

This was the first life lesson he instilled in me: if you want something, you've got to work for it. Or, in this particular case, make your dad work for it. Everything was crafted with his hands and made with so much love. He worked hard to give me the life he envisioned for me, and I will never ever forget that. Sometimes I wonder if he ever felt he had to make up for my mother not being around, but I never missed having a second parent. He was everything I needed and more.

He once said he'd never known someone so stubborn; I felt the same about him. I always had to have the last word, and he often let me. He taught me to speak up for myself and others, and that what I felt, needed or said was important.

My dad gave me the confidence, support and love to achieve anything. It was this strength that helped me navigate his increasing frailty. He was always so strong, I almost believed he was eternal. We remained close throughout my adulthood and it was just me left to watch him slowly slip away. When he passed away, my heart broke.

My father had always been my rock; his life lessons, spirit and support are still with me today, but his passing made my job (working with the elderly and vulnerable) far too painful. I wasn't able to give them the care they deserved. I spent what felt like an eternity in the depths of grief. After many months of gloom, my soul was still recovering and the pain still felt very fresh, but I knew it was time to start trying to move forward. My dad brought me up to keep my head up and to make the most of life; he was such an open-minded man, not afraid to let me find my own path. His death really brought those lessons home to me and so, instead of crumbling, I took on a new challenge and decided to try something new.

I live in Oxfordshire, which is equal parts peaceful countryside and bustling nightlife. Both of these traits fit my personality so well; I'm a real homebody and enjoy the serenity of country life, but I do also love a gin with my friends.

My friends have always been a valued support system, so, when they invited me out to the ballet, I jumped at the chance. I enjoy ballet – something about the mix of drama and passion without any dialogue, which is vastly different from the hustle and bustle of everyday life. It's an opportunity to lose yourself, something I was desperate for.

I didn't know it at the time, but that night was about

to change my life entirely. I knew that I needed to move on, and that this was my time to take all the broken pieces of my spirit and turn them into something amazing. But I didn't know what that looked like until I found myself in a unique and frankly terrifying situation that steered me into this new lane.

After the matinee we went to a Chinese restaurant, and then rounded off the evening with some drinks at a nearby bar. It was one of those evenings where, despite the undertone of sadness, spending time with loved ones, letting my hair down – metaphorically of course, it's far too short for that – helped me feel myself again.

'Clubbing?' Tina winked. The rest of the group were up for it, 'carpe diem' they cheered as I shook my head in disagreement. I had seized the day, but the night was not an option. My cheeks and heart were aching in equal measure – one from laughter and the other from grief. The contradiction of feelings was too much and I felt exhausted. I decided to call it a night, and thanked the girls for a brilliant time.

'Get home safe, Ali!' called Bev as I marched off to the bus stop. I'm used to taking the bus from the city centre back home, to the cottage I share with my family. It takes about twenty minutes and it's a nice bit of time for myself to recharge my social battery.

I glanced up at the digital screen, squinting to make out the lurid yellow letters announcing the next number 6 bus. The glow told me I had eighteen minutes to kill, so

I took a leisurely stroll up and down the aisle of a nearby express supermarket.

I picked up a bottle of water and a mini fruit salad to snack on during the short ride back to my cottage. After tucking my brown leather purse right at the bottom of my bag, I headed out of the shop. Feeling a sudden discomfort at the large group of people who had gathered on the other side of the street, I hitched the strap of my oversized red handbag further onto my shoulder, subtly running my fingers over the zip to ensure it was closed, and, with my elbow pressed tightly against it, I made my way to the stop – now with seven minutes to wait.

The stop is well lit, set about half a metre back from the kerb where the pavement meets the busy road. Usually I would perch myself on the small seats, but today I stood, one eye on the signage and one over the street, as one of the figures made their way towards the bus stop.

'Give me your bag!' a voice bellowed at me. Before I could stop my mouth, I swiftly told him where to go; half proud of standing up for myself and half furious with myself that I was being so bold.

I wasn't aware at this point that the person was holding a small knife. As I clocked it, it lit something in me and I found myself emboldened further.

He lunged at me, with the knife aimed towards my abdomen. *Not today*, I thought to myself, and I launched my bag at his head, knocking the knife from his hand. He swooped down to grab it and swiftly turned on his heel to bolt off in the other direction. My legs, which until then hadn't run a day in their life, took over and I was off after him. He wasn't successful in taking my bag, but he took my security, and the last shred of patience I had left in my body. I was absolutely enraged. I can confidently say my muscles still ache from that unexpected dash, and I'm still incensed.

He turned round and was aghast to see my 5 foot 6 frame on his tail. He ducked down a dark alleyway and, fortunately, common sense kicked in and I stopped, looking up in time to see the number 6 going straight past me.

It's hard to summarise my feelings at that moment. I was infuriated, but more than that I was inspired. What makes a person behave that way? From his attack to my reaction, I was just baffled by his audacity and my instinct for justice.

I called the police and, after a short trip around the city in a police car to try to locate the guy, they took me home. I was disappointed and exhausted.

After the incident, I couldn't stop thinking about it. A man held a knife to me and I was simply not having any of it. I think a more typical reaction would have been one of fear or upset, but it had the opposite effect on me. It made me brave. Then I thought about other people who are subjected to the selfish actions of others, and how defence is not always an option. I decided that I needed to help them.

But what would I do with this newfound passion for doing the right thing? Becoming a vigilante was out of the question. Practicalities aside, I really don't think I've got the physical capabilities. Instead, I started at the very beginning, and began studying psychology. I needed answers and wanted a deeper understanding of the human psyche. I needed to explain the why, not just the what.

As I was always one to do things my way, and of a certain age, a law enforcement career was not an option, but I thought about something law-adjacent. I liked the thrill of the chase – not literally; as I said, my legs are still sore from that night – and the search for answers.

This yearning for knowledge naturally directed me to continue studying until I found something that stuck. I took several courses, one right after the other, including criminology, forensic psychology, profiling and, finally, private investigation.

I was enthralled and astounded by this course. Nothing had lit a fire under me quite like it; I had found my calling.

'I'm going to be a private investigator!' I boldly announced at the dinner table one Sunday. My daughter, Alexis, spoke first, while my husband, Mark, sat there, mouth agape.

'What . . . like . . . Sherlock Holmes?'

'No . . . well . . . sort of? I don't know yet, but I'm going to give it a go,' I told them.

Mark reached across the table and held my hand as he

tried to find the right words. I could tell he thought I was nuts, but he would never say it.

'If anyone can, it's you,' he told me gently.

That night we talked about it for hours. I could tell he was sceptical but I, as always, talked him round, and, in the process, erased any doubt I had in my mind.

I woke up the next morning with what felt like an emotional hangover.

'Good morning, Murder, She Wrote,' Mark joked at me as he presented me my morning cup of tea. I'm ashamed to say I am one of those 'don't talk to me before my cuppa' types, and had a bit of a sulk that he was already mocking my idea. My face said it all, and he immediately apologised for the poorly-timed quip and asked how he could help me pursue my dream.

'I mean . . . how on Earth does someone set up a private investigation business?' I asked, draining my cup.

He shrugged, rather unhelpfully, and I let out a long sigh. I had the qualification thanks to the recent completion of an Open University course, but I had no idea what to do next.

Setting up Miss AM Investigations was the most gut-wrenching, heart-stopping moment of my life. Born from grief, this challenge was significant, and I leapt in with both feet.

I named my business for my dad, choosing to use my maiden name (Marsh) in my professional capacity. I like to think this is a small way to honour the man whose wisdom and support gave me the courage to branch off into an unexpected, daring and fascinating field.

Cut to several years later, I've been dubbed the 'PI who tracks down cheaters' by the *Daily Mail* and *OK!* magazine. Now when I 'go into the office', I never know what to expect. Some cases are straightforward and practical, such as corporate investigations and fraud, and some are emotional or painful cases, such as those involving missing people, cheating spouses or helping to reunite an adopted child with their birth parents. No two days are the same and every case is unique, even if they fall into similar categories. I am constantly learning and improving; every day I become better at what I do and more able to help my clients.

My clients often come to me lost, without the tools they need to help themselves. But, with the qualifications I studied hard for, the experience I have and the tools in my possession, I can help those most vulnerable, providing the support and the results they need.

At its core, the role of a private investigator is to find information that might not otherwise come to light. It's more than likely that this information is only beneficial to one particular party and potentially detrimental to another. From phone taps to honeytraps, there are many unscrupulous ways to close a case, but in order to stay ethical there are certain considerations to be made; I have to navigate a minefield of moral responsibilities.

It's not unheard of for the work of a private investigator

to supplement police investigations. It's important to note the distinctions between the two – the main one being that I have no legal authority. I cannot make use of police resources or access any police records, nor can I put someone under arrest, implement search warrants and so on. I work as a citizen, with a professional certificate in investigation. I am not and will never profess to be an officer of the law.

What I can do, however, is use years of training and experience to uncover information and use information that is available to the public in the quest for the truth for my client.

The overlap often comes when a police investigation is unsuccessful and the person involved chooses to go private instead of using public resources.

There have been times when my investigation has helped the police. Often it is to help ease the pressure by finding out information on their behalf. Any details a PI provides must be verified, but it takes some of the guesswork away from the police. This is typically for missing persons or fraud investigations, but a PI could really help anywhere.

Making the decision to hire a private investigator is a huge step towards finding the truth. Whether it is financial deception, infidelity or business due diligence, there's a set of standards that I live by – it's all about a S.E.C.R.E.T.

Even with all the training in the world, to thoroughly

investigate one needs a strong **Sense of intuition**. Everything must be proven. Without proof there is no culpability, so investigations must be **Evidence-driven**. Proven experience and qualifications make me **Credible**. Investigations can be quite challenging, so I must be **Resilient**. It should be **Easy to talk to me** and I should appear confident and capable within a social setting. And finally, perhaps most importantly, **Trustworthy**.

This set of standards helps me remain ethical in a world of deceit.

I am sharing these cases to showcase the vastness of my chosen career, which is much more involved than simply digging for information. After many years of truth-seeking, I'm still perplexed by the complexity of human behaviour. In most cases, there's a huge aspect of personal trauma that it is my responsibility to help my client navigate, making this career thoroughly rewarding and utterly heart-wrenching in equal measure.

Welcome to my world . . .

CHAPTER 2

Romance Scams

Forty-Five Minutes From the Truth

I'm standing in my kitchen, rubbing my glasses between the folds in my cardigan to remove the steam from my freshly brewed tea and stifling a yawn from another sleepless night. I often find it difficult to drift off at night; something of an occupational hazard. It's not the pressure of cracking a case, or delivering bad news to my clients, that troubles me the most, it's witnessing the despicable lengths people go to in order to hurt each other. One of the reasons I was so interested in this career in the first place was so I could combine my curious nature and love for problem-solving with my desire to help people. But in doing so, I open myself up to their hurt, their heartbreak, and the truly disappointing facets of human nature.

Even our best traits, like love and kindness, are not immune to corruption from our most basic instincts.

As a species, it's written in our DNA to have the desire to continue our legacy. Whether one acts upon this or not is by the by – that is a personal choice, of course – but from an anthropological perspective it's typical for us to want to find a partner.

Historically, pheromones and attractiveness would guide someone towards their ideal mate. They looked for the things they needed to survive – strength, protection and so on; just think of the needs of hunter/gatherer family dynamics. Then travel, particularly international travel, meant that people could look outside their circle for a mate, and then online dating changed the game entirely.

Seemingly thousands of years of human development went out the window and now it's commonplace to allow an algorithm to choose you a partner. Now, I loathe the word algorithm – perhaps mostly because I don't really understand it. I'm quite old school and like a personal touch (metaphorically) when dealing with people.

Sociologist Dr Marie Bergström spent over a decade researching how the dating game has changed and documented her findings in her book titled *The New Laws of Love*. Dr Bergström's book explains that dating has become a private activity and that casual relationships have become much more common than actively seeking a 'soulmate'. The idea that the perfect person for you is out there has removed chance encounters, and instead we are actively seeking a specific person with looks, traits, hobbies and interests that have been selected by preference rather than the instinct for survival. Longevity is not always at the forefront – people don't 'need' a partner, they'd like one and they're willing to go and look for them.

But what happens when finding a match goes wrong? It hurts. What if none of it was real in the first place? Sure, the algorithm can stop you falling for someone with terrible taste in music, but can you really trust it?

I've seen more romance scams than I can count. These fraudulent schemes involve individuals, often operating online, establishing deceptive romantic relationships to exploit victims emotionally and financially. Perpetrators typically create fake profiles on dating websites or social media platforms, cultivating a sense of trust and intimacy with their targets.

The 2022 Netflix true crime documentary *The Tinder Swindler* shone a spotlight on how dating apps like Tinder have opened up new avenues for scammers to find people to exploit. The film, directed by Felicity Morris, tells the story of the Israeli conman Simon Leviev (born Shimon Hayut) who presented himself as the son of Russian-Israeli diamond mogul Lev Leviev and used Tinder to connect with individuals before emotionally manipulating them into financially supporting his lavish lifestyle, on the pretext that he needed the money to escape his so-called enemies.

Leviev would charm his targets with fancy dinners on private jets (paid for by former victims), whisk them away on romantic trips and lavish them with gifts and experiences they might otherwise only dream of. As their relationship grew stronger and the women started to fall for Leviev and trust him, the switch would flip and he would claim that he was under threat from enemies and needed money. Conveniently, due to a 'security risk' he could never access his own funds, so the women dutifully handed over their savings or took out loans and credit cards to help their beloved. Falsified documents would show that he had returned the money via bank transfer, and then he was gone for ever.

I would love to tell you that this is a ridiculous overdramatisation and these things don't really happen. But, unfortunately, cases like this are becoming more frequent. A 2024 investigation by the BBC revealed that reports of romance fraud rose by almost 60 per cent over a four-year period. In England and Wales alone in 2023, 7,660 cases were reported, and I suspect that figure will rise. Leviev's technique is typical of scammers – they lure their targets under false pretences, present a life worth taking a risk for, and then rip it away, leaving devastation in their wake like a hurricane.

I'm experienced in spotting red flags to avoid falling victim to such fraudulent activities, so, when Bradley reached out to me to help him find a man he had fallen for online, I couldn't help but have an immediate sinking feeling.

'I fell in love,' Bradley sighed, with a sheepish look across his pale, bespectacled face, 'and then he disappeared.'

It doesn't take an expert investigator to know there is much, much more to this story.

It was a gloomy Wednesday in February. Pink and red hearts lined the streets in every shop window, contrasting against the misty rain and grey clouds overhead. The cafe where we met was particularly festive with bunting across the ceiling and a single, if not slightly wilted, rose in a small vase on every table, and tiny foil hearts sprawled aimlessly across the pink tablecloths. This was hardly the right setting for a discussion on lost love – an intimate lunch spot in the run-up to Valentine's Day – but it was the only place we could go to get out of the rain, so, rather uncomfortably, we sat and ordered some hot drinks.

I learned that Bradley was a frequent flier on the dating apps. In his words, if you throw enough at the wall, something will stick. He had originally intended on using the apps for brief encounters and had been quite successful.

'I absolutely did not want a boyfriend,' he told me firmly when I asked about his dating history. I needed to get a clear view of his behaviour and intentions before we jumped into the details of the case. 'But then I matched with Alfie.' He inhaled deeply, his chest visibly rising beneath his jumper. He explained that usually he wouldn't swipe on someone who lived far away – they were separated by nearly 250 miles – but something about Alfie's profile photo and bio got his attention.

'We liked all the same things and he was utterly

gorgeous!' he said, swooning. He told me about his love of film, music and Japanese food – all things that Alfie also loved. This made my ears prick up, as these are very broad interests that are typically used as conversation starters to establish a connection, before mining for more information – it's the perfect in. We like the same generic things, what are the chances! I stifled an eye-roll. This wasn't Bradley's fault; these scammers are experts at this sort of thing.

'I knew it wouldn't be just a fling; I was immediately hooked by him.' He showed me a photo of a muscular, tanned blond man on a beach. It looked like he'd waded into the ocean on some luxurious island and turned back casually right as someone took a photo. The waves were hugging against his thighs, lapping against his black tight shorts. It was the perfect candid – even I had a small swoon. 'That's Alfie . . . at least I really really hope it is.' The desperation in his voice was palpable; his heartache echoed in the small wobble in his voice. 'I'm so scared that I've been catfished.'

Bradley was referring, of course, to the 2010 documentary thriller *Catfish*, which followed Nev Schulman as he tried to find the true identity of the person he fell for online after a series of troubling inconsistencies left him asking questions. In the film, Nev coins the term 'catfish' to describe a person who strings someone along, explaining the theory that, when live cod were shipped from North America to Asia, they would become lethargic and their flesh would become mushy. To prevent this, some clever fishermen would place catfish in the tanks with the cod to keep them active and alert during the journey. In this context, however, the term 'catfish' is used to describe someone who keeps another person alert and active in a relationship by creating a false persona.

I learned that Alfie started the conversation by asking lots of questions about Bradley. He wasn't used to app users actually caring; usually the chat was a little more straightforward, with a clear goal in mind.

Bradley handed me his phone to show me their first few exchanges, and Alfie seemed genuinely interested in him. His questions were inquisitive and friendly – he came across as being really warm and genuine. If Alfie was a scammer, he seemed to know all of the tricks. But, it was far too early to tell, the red flags could be explained away quite easily, so I chose to give them both the benefit of the doubt . . . for the time being.

Reading through their conversations, I saw Bradley talking passionately about his family and how important they were to him.

'We lost my grandparents when I was 20,' one of the exchanges read. 'They both died in a care home, Pops first, then Nanna just 3 weeks later.' He explained how the staff at the home were so kind to his family and that he was a regular fundraiser for the charity that ran it, and that people who work in care were saints in his eyes.

'Oh sweetheart!' Alfie responded. 'That's devastating,

I'm so sorry you went through that. I understand, I actually stopped working a few months ago to take care of my mum as she's unwell, so I really respect that you still donate money to the cause.' Followed by several heart emojis.

'I was blown away,' Bradley recalled. 'I'd never connected with someone who'd had a similar experience and cared so deeply. I knew at that moment I was starting to fall for him – I know that sounds silly!' I assured him that he did not sound silly. In fact, he sounded like almost everyone who comes to me with this sort of case. Unbeknown to Bradley, by sharing this detail about his family he gave Alfie exactly what he needed to make a deep connection.

Bradley went on to tell me more about their blossoming romance and why he needed my help. After three failed attempts to meet, Alfie disappeared.

'Half of me is worried that something is wrong. I'm trying to give him the benefit of the doubt but I'm losing hope.' Well, actually he said, 'benny of the d', which my daughter translated for me. Not one previously in my vernacular, but every day is a school day! I made a note to add that to my millennial dictionary.

'We were voice-noting one night,' Bradley said, 'and I mentioned I would be in South London for a festival in a few weeks.' He told me that Alfie was going to the same festival and would 'love to meet up'. However, he was going to be with a huge group of friends so may not be able to.

'I couldn't believe my luck! He'd never mentioned liking this sort of thing before, so I was surprised, but pleased.' I did all I could to keep my eyebrow firmly in place and just raised it mentally. Funny how they already supposedly had so much in common, and yet something as pivotal as music taste hadn't come up. I added this to my list of inconsistencies that littered Bradley's recollections of Alfie.

The weekend of the festival arrived and they'd arranged to meet up to see a few different acts, if Alfie's friends were okay with it. Sadly, due to Alfie saying that he lost his phone on the first night of the festival, they weren't able to connect.

'I'm so sorry darling', 'please forgive me', 'I promise to make it up to you'. . . and so on, read the messages from after the weekend.

'I was gutted, but it's just one of those things,' said Bradley with a shrug. 'He promised to make it up to me, so he arranged to travel to my town in the next few weeks.'

I'm not a cynic and I do genuinely believe people can find love on these apps, but from what I'd learned so far, coupled with Alfie being MIA, I knew what he'd say next.

Alfie's mum took a turn for the worse, so he had to take her into hospital on the very weekend he was meant to travel down to see Bradley. I didn't want Bradley to know that I sadly felt that I knew where this story was going, so I maintained absolute interest in what he had to say and echoed his hopes for finally meeting Alfie, despite experience telling me how unlikely it was.

'I was absolutely crushed! Part of me wondered if it was true but he sent me a selfie as proof.' He handed me his phone. There was a photo of Alfie outside blue double doors with an illuminated 'Accident and Emergency' sign above his head and a bright blue light shining from a nearby ambulance. 'He was obviously at the hospital, and look' – he thrust the phone at me again – 'look how sad he looks!' Bradley looked at the photo and sighed with dejection; I looked at it and sighed with the crushing weight of knowing what would come next.

The following day, Bradley told me, a huge bunch of flowers and a teddy bear arrived at his door. The card read, 'Please forgive me love, my mum needs me right now but our time will come – please don't give up on me.' He visibly swooned as he told me.

'I didn't give up on him. I couldn't . . . but then . . .' Bradley's eyes watered slightly and he fell silent for a few moments, lost in his thoughts. I reached across the tacky tablecloth to gently pat his arm in sympathy and encourage him to go on.

Just then, the server came over and asked if we wanted anything else, which broke Bradley's trance. I ordered a peppermint tea and Bradley asked if they served cocktails. I couldn't help but chuckle. I really liked him and I was becoming more and more saddened by his story.

I knew it was coming; but the small glimmer of hope that this might be different and that the cynic in me was overreacting was swiped away when Bradley told me the next part of the story.

'He'd already told me he quit his job to care for his mum, so when he told me he had arranged for someone else to stay with her so we could meet up, but he needed some help with the train fare, I jumped at the chance!'

Do you ever just hate being right? You couldn't have written a more textbook case of romance scams. Reel them in – disappoint – love-bomb – disappoint – make them feel sorry for you – ask for money.

'He told me it was cheaper for him to book tickets in advance, but he just didn't have the cash right now. What he said – £150 – seemed about reasonable for a train from York to Kent, but it would be over £300 if he waited until his carer's allowance came in.'

Some might say foolishly, Bradley sent him the money. I can understand why; I've seen it happen too many times. Without judgement, I listened as Bradley explained that once money changed hands, everything changed.

Firstly, Alfie's mannerisms changed, there were fewer 'babe's and 'sweetheart's. 'He called me Brad! I hate being called Brad and he knows that, so it really rattled me!'

Shortly after sending the money, Alfie sent confirmation of his purchased train tickets, but then the conversations dwindled, then stopped entirely. Bradley showed me a printout of the screenshot Alfie had sent him. It looked legitimate enough, but image editing software can be so convincing, it was hard to be sure.

'He didn't turn up, he didn't answer any of my texts or calls, he just disappeared. So, while I probably shouldn't admit it, I was rather drunk at the time, as I needed some Dutch courage before I asked for help. I felt embarrassed, still do to be honest, but I was – am – desperate for answers.'

I'd replied to Bradley's message as soon as I received it, as I often do, which he told me was unexpected. I said, if he didn't really want to connect with me, why did he meet with me today?

'Because you seemed like you genuinely cared and I didn't want to waste your time . . . so here we are. Can you find him?' he pleaded. I've spoken to many prospective clients and none have ever been quite as honest as Bradley. It was refreshing, and slightly concerning, so I reiterated some of the rules and what Bradley should expect from an investigation of this sort.

'I'll be upfront,' I told him. 'Investigations are costly, time-consuming, and can be very emotionally taxing. I don't want to take you down this path if you are not entirely sure.' I explained that in my experience cases like this are pretty cut and dried, and from the top I didn't believe this to be Bradley's happily-ever-after – as much as I would have loved to be wrong.

'I'm absolutely positive. Let's do it.'

He nodded firmly and I believed he was truly ready for

closure. So, after a little more talking, I agreed to have a preliminary snoop and then we parted ways.

I walked towards my car, pausing to notice that the rain had calmed down and a sliver of blue skies peeked behind the storm clouds. I try to travel by public transport as much as possible, as it gives me a chance to reflect on the case and look over my notes while it's all still fresh in my mind. Unfortunately, on this occasion rail strikes had forced me to drive, so I spent the two-and-a-half-hour trip recording my thoughts into my Dictaphone.

I hadn't formally accepted the case yet; I like to go over my notes and have a good think about things before I commit completely. It's one of my worst nightmares to tell a client that I can help when it turns out I actually can't. It's happened to me before, albeit rarely.

When I got back to my cottage, the sun was shining and it seemed the gloomy rain of Kent hadn't made it over to Oxfordshire yet. The forecast indicated storms that evening, so I decided to unwind a bit by taking the dog for a long walk over the fields before the inclement weather hit.

I slung my scruffy jacket over my shoulders – the one specifically for dog walking – and grabbed the leash and my young-at-heart, old-in-legs dear old boy Barry. As we walked up the lane, lined with spindly twigs ravaged by winter where the usually bountiful shrubbery grew, I steeled myself to listen to my voice notes. If there is one thing I hate, it is the sound of my own voice. I'm often called upon to do radio interviews discussing my career, but I couldn't tell you what I've said in any of them as I outright refuse to listen! So, hesitantly, I popped my earbuds in and turned down the dusty path to the field.

'Well, Alfie sounds like a right toerag,' boomed my voice. I chuckled and reminded myself not to make snap judgements, despite the evidence clearly indicating that Alfie was not who he said he was. I walked with Barry until the sun began to dip below the hills and the cold began to set in. All six legs on this walk were cold and tired, and I couldn't stand to listen to the notes anymore, so we hotfooted it home.

The Hunt Begins

Looking back over my notes and listening to the recordings I'd made in the car, I was fairly sure how this case was going to go. The red flags were stacking up and it seemed like Alfie was working a pattern that is extremely common with scammers.

I decided it was the right time to get back in touch with Bradley, and agreed to take the case. We had the awkward conversation about price and he agreed. 'I'm already £150 down, I just want to get the answers I deserve,' he boldly proclaimed. I discussed my initial impressions with him and he sounded so sad when I said that, while I had absolutely no proof yet, some of Alfie's actions were concerning. We hung up and I hoped I could give him closure as soon as possible.

My first step was to establish some legitimacy for the character of Alfie. Was he a real person who had made a mistake? Was he entirely false? It wasn't clear at this point, so I went straight to the place with all the answers – Alfie's socials.

Bradley sent me links to the accounts on which he had connected with Alfie. While they met on a dating app, they also connected on Instagram and Snapchat.

The Instagram profile for Alfie had a generic username, 'Alf_99', and was full of photos of scenic holiday spots, plus a football pitch, which the caption tells me was taken at York City FC vs Dagenham and Redbridge, as well as a selfie of him in the stands. No one else apart from the teams was tagged in the photo, which I noticed was the same for all of his posts – no friends were tagged at all, but locations were.

There were several photos of Alfie himself, including some of the ones from his dating profile and some of the more 'personal' photos that he had sent to Bradley, which had been carefully cropped at the hips. Bradley showed me some of the intimate pictures that Alfie had sent him but tactfully held his thumb over the lower third of the screen. In case you can't infer what I mean, I'm talking about rather explicit nudes. The images on his profile were the same shots, without the NSFW parts.

The bio didn't give anything away regarding location, sexuality, relationship status or hobbies. It simply read 'Alfie's Insta – loving life' and, from the photos, it looked like he was! I could see why Bradley was drawn to him. He came across as a really interesting guy, well travelled as shown by his photos of Spain, Greece, America, Scotland and more, and with a very active social life. From the profile alone, he seemed like a legitimate person, but I knew I needed to look deeper than that.

He had several hundred followers, but only two or three likes on each photo, and generic comments from the same profiles saying things like, 'looks good mate', 'have a safe trip' and so on. There were no clues . . . which in itself is a huge clue.

One of my mantras is that you can find out more by what isn't said than by what is, and that is something that applied here when I was looking at Alfie's profile. It was all flash, no substance. With several hundred friends, why was there so little engagement? It simply wasn't adding up.

I dug deeper into the accounts that interacted with his posts and saw that they were all private profiles, no bios, and faceless photos. I knew this was a common trick of people setting up fake profiles – they make several anonymous profiles and interact with the main account to make it look like a real person. Scam businesses often do this; they create fake customers to comment on their Facebook posts and give positive reviews, when in fact it's all just bought promotion. It was safe to assume that most of Alfie's followers were bought – either bots, or fake accounts he'd created himself – and I wondered where the real Alfie was hiding.

My next trick was to add Alfie's number to WhatsApp and see how his profile showed up on there, using my burner phone, which I use purely for anonymously looking people up. There was no profile picture and no name, so I sent a message:

'Hi, this is Angela, we met at the DIY shop today. Hoping you can help me out with an estimate for my renovations – let me know when it's convenient to chat!'

This is a classic PI trick. Go in pretending to be someone else to get their attention, and if they respond you can say you must have the wrong number. I waited for the two ticks to show me the message had been received, but even after fifteen minutes there was still just one, indicating that this number was not active. I made a note to check back on this later, but I didn't hold out much hope.

I needed a break but I still had a bit of fire in my belly to get some more information, so before I called it a night I stepped away from looking into Alfie and instead spent some time understanding Bradley a bit more.

Obviously I had spoken to Bradley in depth, so I had a good idea of the sort of character he was, but I needed to see more of his online persona. It's not uncommon to find that someone's online characteristics are entirely different from their real self. I was quite relieved to see that Bradley appeared just as confident, funny, thoughtful and kind online as he did in person. He was, for lack of a better term, a cheeky chap. He loved socialising; his grid was full of photos of him having fun with big groups of people.

It stood out to me that Bradley was not your typical mark. More often, the people targeted by scammers are openly looking for love or companionship – in other words, they're lonely and they need something that the perpetrator can give them. Bradley didn't fit this bill, which might be why it had seemed less suspicious when someone swooped in portraying the perfect match.

This said more about Alfie than Bradley. 'He's good at this,' I sighed to myself.

It can be so easy for me to spot the red flags in these behaviours that sometimes my impression of my client can become a bit cloudy. I'm a bit ashamed to admit that, while I always have the utmost respect for my clients and sympathy for their plight, sometimes I struggle to understand why people fall for scams like this. At these times I need to remind myself that it's not always obvious to those who haven't had the training and experience that someone like me has.

It had been a few days since I spoke to Bradley and I really wanted to give him answers, but I simply didn't have them yet. There were a few bites but nothing concrete. Hours of poring over social media is exhausting, so I decided it was time to have a bit of a breather and time away from the small screen . . . and instead turned on the big screen and settled into some chewing-gum TV.

Relaxing is quite difficult for me, especially in the middle of a case. I find it hard to switch off when I know people are counting on me.

Sensing my stress, my husband brought me a G&T and a bowl of crisps, and loaded *The Blues Brothers* up on the television. It's one of my absolute favourites – a story of redemption and family, alongside outlandish obstacles and marvellous music. It's something I can get lost in when I'm feeling tightly wound. I'm not one for romcoms, especially when working on a case like this. After the film – during which I fell asleep halfway through, shortly after the 'Think' sequence – I climbed the stairs and flopped into bed.

With a fresh outlook, I jumped back on the case the following morning, starting with a reverse image search on Alfie's photos. There were no hits that weren't related to the social media pages I already had looked into. This wasn't a huge shock, as the variety of images available across various platforms, especially the explicit photos with very specific requested details, led me to believe that Alfie is a real person and those are his photos, but it is unclear what – if any – of his story is true.

I searched his name on Facebook and no profile matching Alfie's picture came up, which is also suspicious as, typically, if someone has Instagram they'll have Facebook too. I looked through the profiles with similar names but no photographs, looking for anything to tie them to the case.

Nothing stood out in the seven profiles I checked, so I started trying to tie things to Alfie's profile, recalling the photos from York City FC vs Dagenham and Redbridge. Now I would rather stick needles in my eyes than watch football, but, ever the professional, I read up about both teams and learned that they were in the same league and had played each other at Dagenham a few days before the photo was posted on Alfie's profile.

Looking up location tags from around that time, I found a chap called Alfie Underwood, who was tagged in a photo by someone called Laurence Willis. Comparing the photo on Laurence's profile to the one on Alfie's Instagram, I could see a resemblance between him and someone in the crowd near Alfie. It wasn't a definite match, but the dates matched up, as did many other aspects of both images. Could this be our Alfie? The page was private and I couldn't delve more, so instead I trawled through the football team's pages.

I searched York City FC's website and socials for more comments from Alfie Underwood but nothing came up. I searched forums, fan pages, and even the profiles of the players. Nothing.

Then, a lightbulb moment.

Alfie said he was from York, and there were pictures of him at York City FC vs Dagenham. Was that a red herring? It was clear he was at the game, but what if he was on the other side?

I gasped, putting down my cup of tea and leaning back in my black leather chair. It squeaked in protest and Barry, who is aways nestled by my toes, pricked up an ear and looked at me with disgust for daring to disturb his snooze.

I held my chin in my hands and leaned forward again, resting on the desk. Thoughts were darting around my head and I felt my body shoot into high alert.

I needed to do the exact same search but not for York: for Dagenham and Redbridge.

'If you've been forty-five minutes away this whole time, Alfie . . .' I said out loud.

'Who's Alfie?' My daughter nosed round my office door. I heard her, but I was so transfixed by this sudden wave of inspiration that I completely ignored her. She's definitely used to it by now – once I'm in the zone, everything else is just white noise.

I searched, and searched, and searched some more across dozens of pages. I zoomed into photos of fans, searching for Alfie's face. I read at least fifty threads on a fan forum, looking for his name or anything similar. I read so much about football I thought my brain was going to explode – until I found myself on the Official Daggers TV YouTube channel.

The top comment on a recent video introducing a new player was from a profile of someone called 'A_Dagger_U'. I clapped my hands together (annoying Barry once again) and took a deep breath. Private profile. Damn. I wasn't ready to give up this line of inquiry, so I searched the username in the forums.

A_Dagger_U had a profile. With a photo.

'GOT YOU!' I cheered as I looked into the eyes of the Alfie I'd been looking for. The Alfie that charmed Bradley into handing over his money.

Alfie Underwood.
27.
Die-hard Daggers fan 4 lyf.
Live in Essex with my gf.

Closure Time

It was all a lie, I had been pretty convinced it was, but here was the proof. I was devastated for Bradley, and I knew the next part – telling him – would be so hard.

I emailed him saying I was ready to meet again. Wednesday, midday, same place. He reminded me that it would in fact be Valentine's Day and, given the state of the place last time we were there, we decided on Thursday instead. That gave me two days to gather the evidence and compile a report.

I don't like to share findings over the phone – I had told Bradley this when I first took the case, so he kindly didn't press me for information before our meeting. But I think he knew deep down he wasn't getting his happy ending.

Being able to give my client closure is the most satisfying yet solemn part of the job. It's hard to crush someone's dreams but it's my responsibility to tell the truth.

'Oh,' was all Bradley said. He sat there for quite some time just staring at the documents I presented to him.

He didn't even appear to be reading them; just looking at them willing the words to change.

'I'm really sorry, Bradley,' I said, reaching my hand across the table, no longer laden with Valentine's tat. The bunting was gone too; just empty space hung above our heads, as if it was mocking us. Neither of us really knew what to say, but his hurt was palpable.

'I just don't understand why someone would do this to anyone, but especially to me. I haven't done anything to anyone; no one deserves to be treated this way.' His cheeks reddened and his eyes misted with emotion. He sniffed, wiped his left eye with the sleeve of his blue hoodie and took a deep breath.

'In this instance, there's no way to know for sure . . .' I began, preparing myself for the big question. 'Unless you want me to ask him?' I paused, trying to gauge his answer before he spoke. Sometimes when I ask this the client's interest is piqued and I know to ask again. But Bradley looked down and slowly shook his head.

'Are you absolutely sure?' I asked.

'Yes. A hundred per cent. I don't want to know whatever stupid excuse he has for doing such a hideous thing. I never want to hear the name Alfie' – he paused to check the documents in front of him – 'Underwood again. I am so done with this storyline of my life, and that thieving turd doesn't get any more of my time or energy.'

I wanted to high-five him across the table, but, ever the professional, I simply said, 'Okay'.

After chatting about the case and life in general for about an hour over coffee and cake, we went our separate ways. He thanked me for giving him closure and I said it was a pleasure getting to know him. It really was; he was a really nice person and I hoped that this experience didn't change that, but gave him a little insight into how to be safe online.

I'd asked him once more if he wanted me to reach out to the real Alfie, but he declined. He just wanted to move on and put the last six months behind him. I respected his decision, and closed the case on Alfie Underwood.

PI Perspective

I don't want my work to put people off the pursuit of happiness – it is out there and it can be found online. It's just essential to act safely. There are effective ways to avoid something like this happening to you.

The motivation behind a catfish can vary; it could be to exploit someone financially – as with Bradley's story – or it could be a way to get closer to someone they think might not otherwise be interested, or simply out of revenge or boredom. And that makes it even scarier. It sounds dramatic, but unfortunately these cases are real and especially prevalent today.

There are several major red flags that can give away when someone online is not being truthful about their motive or identity. If you're feeling uncomfortable about the person you are talking to, you should always stop communicating, period. If you're not sure whether you are dealing with a catfish, here are some behaviours to look out for – you may have clocked most of these in Bradley's case.

A lot can be inferred from what a person is saying, as well as when and how they say it. Things to look out for include astonishing life stories (like the Tinder Swindler's lavish lifestyle that was actually afforded by scamming countless women), mirroring your circumstances and/ or life experiences (for example in Bradley's case, they bonded over sick relatives), or catching them in a lie and them finding an elaborate but irrefutable excuse.

Other common red flags include last-minute cancell-ation of plans, repeated bouts of sickness or family issues, hints or outright requests for money or gifts that will benefit you in some undisclosed way, or demanding acts of love or service to show your loyalty.

There are many techniques to prevent you from falling prey to a catfish. They might seem obvious from the outside, but these people are very skilled at lulling people into a false sense of security and preying on any weakness, and can get inside a person's head.

Firstly (and actually this applies to life in general), you should protect your social media presence. In order for a catfish to lure you in, you first have to take the bait. A catfish will typically approach you via social media, so to remove the risk simply make your social media accounts private. Any would-be catfish will not be able to glean any details about you before they reach out, making it harder for them to make that integral connection.

Fully investigate any friend requests you receive. If you don't know them directly, check how many mutual friends you have with them. If there are many but no clear connection between them all, there's a chance the profile isn't genuine. If at all unsure, decline the request.

The catfish MO is picking up on small details about their target to form a bond. This could be shared experiences such as losing a loved one, surviving some sort of traumatic event, or even simply having similar hobbies. They will ask you questions to get to know you, while revealing little about themselves. This might make them come across as caring and attentive, but really it is a smokescreen, which is easy to fall for. If you do end up in a conversation with someone you don't know, keep your cards close to your chest. Make sure you ask them detailed, original questions, rather than encouraging them to give their answer to whatever they have asked you.

Messaging services are great, but they're so one-dimensional it makes it easy to pretend to be someone else, so try connecting on several different platforms to establish their legitimacy.

Phone calls and video calls are a sure-fire way to get more info about a person. Do they look like their photo? If you can only chat through audio, consider the sound of their voice – do they sound male or female? Do they have an accent that matches what they've told you? If they refuse to connect this way, or constantly come up with excuses why not to, then that is a huge red flag.

If you personally prefer to communicate via written message, then you can choose apps that give you a little more protection. For example, WhatsApp requires a mobile number (most other services need just a username and email address, which can be spoofed). A catfish is unlikely to give out their mobile number, and if they do you can do a reverse look-up to get some information about the user.

You can also look up numbers by searching on Facebook. A while ago, Facebook encouraged all users to add a mobile number and, while you can set it to not show on your account, the information does still exist in the back end of your profile. Searching a number on Facebook can show you the profile it is linked to – which may not be the person you think it is.

They've likely used your social media to find out more about you – you can do the same to them! Things to look out for include:

- How long the profile has been active – if it was created recently, it's likely to be a fake.
- Their friends list – a small number of connections can hint at them not being legitimate.
- How much they interact online – check if they have joined any groups, liked pages or interacted

with others. The more engagement, the more likely they are real.

- Tagged photos – check if anyone else has tagged them in photos or posts.

Legalities

Campaigners are constantly calling for the government or police to intervene to help stop the plight of catfishers' victims. There are currently several regulations in force to help combat catfishing, such as the Malicious Communications Act of 1988, which is a British Act of Parliament that makes it illegal in England and Wales to 'send or deliver letters or other articles for the purpose of causing distress or anxiety'. The Act also applies to electronic communications. A person found guilty of this offence is liable to a fine or up to twelve months' imprisonment.

It's likely we had enough proof for Bradley to have used this Act to seek justice, but he felt closure was enough and chose to move on.

I can't say for sure what would have happened, but I'm pleased to have closed the case with a satisfied – if heartbroken – client.

CHAPTER 3

Leads for Leads

Imaginary Pooch Saves the Day

When you think of the archetypal private investigator, I'm sure you imagine all kinds of fancy gadgets. But if you delve deeper into those fictional characters, you'll learn that most of them simply rely on their brains and a notebook.

Sherlock Holmes, Nancy Drew, Sam Spade, Jessica Fletcher . . . They all have these things in common: impeccable intellect, a thirst for knowledge and relentless note-taking. (They also often feature interesting hats and a cigarette, but let's gloss over that). Hercule Poirot – arguably one of the most famous literary PIs – often credits his solves to his 'little grey cells'.

So to say my brain is my biggest tool would be accurate, but secretly I have a whole kit full of indispensable items to help me solve a case.

I don't profess to be an expert in espionage with an arsenal full of secret gadgets that I use for clandestine purposes. Instead, my kit is full of useful, practical items. Some may be expected, such as a camera, Dictaphone, dashcam, notepad and pen, but some are not so predictable.

I use a set of innocuous items that allow me to explain my presence in an area I'm surveilling, or to give me a way to strike up a conversation with someone without causing suspicion.

The item that is the most time-consuming to keep accurate is a folder full of leaflets. Every new place I visit, the first thing I'll do is pop into a local leisure centre, post office or similar, and grab a handful of various leaflets for different services such as takeaways. I also have a huge selection of nationwide businesses like double-glazers, flooring specialists and more.

My favourite item is a pair of boots, with one heel broken. Slipping those on gives me a reason to sit somewhere for a long time, saying, 'My friend is on her way with a pair of trainers,' if anyone asks if I am okay'. This has only happened once, and I was asked by the person I was watching and it was a fantastic conversation opener. This was coupled with my most advantageous tool to get out of sticky situations – the gift of the gab.

The least suspect item in my kit is a dog lead. The brown strap has been well used, and the fraying edges round the clasp indicate the potential for a breakout.

This lives in my kit alongside a tatty dog-walking jacket and a pocket full of pup treats. This valuable tool was just what I needed to catch a cheater in the act.

Usually when people reach out to me to see if their partner is cheating, they're heartbroken, and a little bit desperate. They've reached the end of their tether and they simply need to know.

When Jeanette contacted me, she didn't seem heartbroken. She was livid.

'I will not have him make a fool out of me anymore!' she spat. 'Five years wasted, and I'm just done.'

Jeanette and Colin were together for two years before tying the knot, five years before she reached out to me. She told me that, from the moment they were introduced by mutual friends, they knew they'd end up together. Their values, morals and life goals were perfectly aligned and they seemed like the perfect match.

After her initial email, which outlined why she suspected him of cheating, we met up at a coffee shop near where she lived in Abingdon – a convenient eight miles from where I live in Oxford.

I always get to my meet-ups a little before my potential client. I like to watch them as they enter, to read their body language and try to catch their vibe. This is a good way to tell if they're genuine or masking when they meet me.

We arranged to meet at 10:30am, so at 10:15 I walked into the coffee shop, ordered a tea, strong with one sugar, then grabbed a table near the back but with a view of the counter and the door.

I was sipping my tea when, at 10:31, the door pinged open. In walked a tall, confident-looking woman with long blond hair. Her face was striking, with soft features, pale pink glasses and lipstick to match. She looked exactly like the photos I had seen while checking her social media before the meeting. She was dressed immaculately in tight-fitting black jeans, a loose crop top and an absolutely stunning long faux-fur leopard-print coat that I desperately wanted for myself. I made a mental note to check out the label to see where it was from.

She looked around and the confidence she had when she walked in began to slip away as she searched for my face in the crowd. She suddenly seemed vulnerable, then relieved when I popped my head up over the crowd and beckoned her over.

'Hi Ali, it's great to meet you.' She beamed at me, shaking my hand vigorously. 'I'll just grab a coffee before we chat – can I get you anything?' I already had my tea, so she walked over to the counter and I saw her take a deep breath and a long exhale. She seemed nervous and the bravado she had shown initially was slipping fast.

'I'll be honest, I feel sick about this,' she admitted when she sat down. 'I was so sure when we first spoke on the phone, but now I think I'm just being ridiculous. Something is definitely up, and I really do think he's cheating, but I don't know if I'm handling this all wrong.'

'You're not the first person to feel this way upon meeting,' I reassured her. I would never persuade or coax someone into using a service they didn't really need. All I could do was talk to her and see if I could help. 'Let's just chat about it all, and see how you feel. No pressure.'

She seemed relieved, and took another steadying breath.

'Ok . . . where to start?'

'Well, tell me about you and your husband.'

She told me they'd met at a birthday party for a mutual friend.

'Holly told me she had a friend who I would just love, and she was right. She introduced me and Colin and there was an immediate connection. Our chemistry was on fire, we really hit it off right away and he seemed like the perfect fit for me and my life.'

She explained that both she and Colin were very career driven. She worked in public relations, in a senior position in a top firm in London, and he was a senior financier for a bank, working with companies across the globe.

'Funnily enough, my firm represented his, so it's weird our paths hadn't crossed before. We'd been to the same event a few weeks before we actually met. We said it was bizarre that we'd been so close but hadn't met until the time was right.' She looked really sad for a split second, then she steadied herself and said: 'Then he ballsed all that up!'

'Jeanette, you don't have to put on any kind of front with me. I just want you to know that anything you say is completely safe with me. I've dealt with more cases like this than I can count, so don't feel like you have to force yourself to be strong – it's okay to be sad.'

And with that, the floodgates opened. She sobbed and sobbed on my shoulder, saying she couldn't believe he would do this to her. I felt devastated for her. I had no idea if he was cheating or not at this point, but she was just so sad, I knew I wanted to get closure for her.

'Ugh!' she sighed. 'I hate feeling like this, it's so not me to be whimpering over a stupid man but I just feel so bloody lost.'

'Do you feel able to tell me why you feel like he is cheating? What started it off?'

'Well, our marriage is somewhat unconventional; we don't actually live together, never have.'

I was taken aback, and it must have shown on my face because she immediately tried to explain. I know a lot of couples do things their own way, but I'd never met a couple married for so many years not living together.

'It's not weird or anything, we're just so stubborn and set in our ways. We argued for months about whose house to live in and neither of us wanted to relent. We trialled it for a while in each house and even looked at houses in the middle ground, but just found that we were happiest when we had our own place and our own space. When we'd get together over the weekends it was perfect. I think it helped keep the spark alive for a lot longer than it might have if we'd moved in together. It's different, but it works for us.' She took a pause. 'Worked for us.'

I asked how, if they were living separate lives, things had changed now to make her suspicious.

'He's just not about anymore. Physically or emotionally. He's always working over the weekends, so he said there's no point coming all the way to mine or me going all the way to his house for him to not be there. He turned his location off on his phone, which he has never done before. I surprised him at work on his lunch break and he smelt like perfume – said he had a meeting with all women but I had checked his diary and there was nothing in it. It's loads of little things like that. He's changed and I don't trust him anymore.'

'A lot of these behaviours can be explained by other things. Have you tried talking to him about how you feel?'

'Yeah, he just shuts me down. Says I'm being stupid. He said half the reason he married me is because I don't ask stupid questions and I let him get on with his life. That's true, but I didn't mean I wouldn't care if he had a different one!'

'How did those comments make you feel?'

'Like a prize prat, to be honest. It just inflamed my suspicions – he's doing something behind my back . . . Or someone.' She rolled her eyes – I think half at what she said, and half at the fact that she had to say it.

I told her that a lot of these things can be explained away, but they are red flags, and typically things I would look into.

'So . . . what shall we do about it?' I asked.

She chewed her pink-glossed lip and picked at her manicured nails. She didn't speak for a while, but she looked me right in the eyes the whole time. I matched her steely look as if to say, 'I've got this.'

She closed her eyes and when she opened them she was looking down. Her blond hair fell around her face as if shielding her from the pain. I was sure she was going to walk away but she lifted her head confidently, tossed her locks over her shoulder and said: 'Catch the bastard.'

After talking a while longer, including the necessary conversation around contracts and fees, Jeanette and I parted ways with a step-by-step plan to see what Colin was really up to on those working weekends.

The plan was to follow him from work on a Friday evening to see if he was really heading home or going somewhere else. After establishing where he was going, I would conduct surveillance on the address and try to catch evidence of him cheating – or whatever else he was doing. Sounds simple enough, but, as always, things are never straightforward. I had to wait for a weekend when Colin said he was unable to see Jeanette due to work, so it would be a few weeks before I could begin the investigation.

I preface this next part by saying I never have used and never will use a so-called honeytrap to prove infidelity.

A honeytrap is a method used by unscrupulous private investigators to catch cheaters or gather evidence of infidelity. This technique typically involves setting up a situation in which one person is intentionally made to believe they are being pursued or desired by an attractive individual, in order to see how they behave. The aim of a honeytrap is to lure the subject in, get them to succumb, and thereby prove that they're capable of cheating.

An investigator can either be the honeytrap themselves or employ someone to play the part. This individual is typically selected based on the target's known preferences, and over time the accomplice continues engaging with the subject to try to get them to act. This might involve suggestive comments, flirtation, or even an upfront invitation.

If the target falls for the trap, the honey discreetly collects evidence of infidelity, such as recording conversations, taking photos or videos, or observing their behaviour to document actions that prove inappropriate conduct.

This is not a way that I believe a good investigator should conduct themselves. Firstly, this only proves someone *would* cheat, not that they are cheating. I investigate actions, not intentions. Secondly, this method is wildly unethical and potentially illegal.

Now that's out of the way, I can explain my next steps. I have a secret dating app account – don't worry, my husband is aware of this. I only ever use it briefly, just to see if my subject is using the app. I never engage, it's purely research. I used a VPN to change my location to where Colin lived and have a little search through. I didn't spend a long time doing this – it could take days of swiping to find the right person. I put the task aside after an hour.

I then reverse image searched Colin's photo to see if he had any social media accounts I'm not already aware of. Colin had no social media at all, fake or genuine. So this investigation would be purely practical, with no social snooping required. It's refreshing to have a case like this; often many hours are spent trawling through a person's online persona to find little threads to pull on.

A few weeks passed and I busied myself with other jobs, making sure to leave my Friday evenings free should Jeanette call upon me. Then, on a rainy Wednesday, Jeanette sent me a screenshot captioned with 'It's go time!'

The screenshot showed a WhatsApp exchange between Colin and Jeanette. It read:

> So sorry, J, work is bonkers this week, I'm going to have to spend the weekend stuck in the office or working at home, then probably off to Frankfurt on Monday. Hopefully back to normal for the following weekend. Sorry x

> Again?! Please Colin, we never get time together any more. Can't I tag along or wait for you at home?

> You know how it is, won't be there so no point.

Isn't the point that we want
to spend time together?

Well that's just how it is

Blimey, what a lovely chap he is, I thought to myself.

I replied to Jeanette that I was on the case, and made the plans for Friday.

When Friday rolled around, I was raring to go. I love a practical investigation: the anticipation, the mystery and the (metaphorical) getting my hands dirty is so thrilling. Colin's home was a little west of London, and his office was in central London. Jeanette told me that he would drive about twenty minutes to a local train station that took him right into the centre, so my plan was to wait at the station and follow him from there. This was much easier than following him all the way from his offices by tube or by car – if you've ever navigated London on a Friday evening, you'll know it would be almost impossible to keep following.

I parked at the station at 4pm, knowing it would likely be at least an hour before Colin's arrival, but I didn't want to risk him leaving early and missing him. At about 5:40, I spotted him leaving the station and heading to his car – a silver Mercedes C-Class with 71 plates, from 2001. It was a gorgeous car and it went well with his tall frame in a sharp suit.

He sat there for a few minutes with the engine idling, so I started my engine and waited. The trick with following in a car is to not get too close, so I waited a beat after he left the car park before heading off myself. Before I knew it, we were on the M4 heading away from the city. It was 6pm when we hit the motorway, and slow traffic the whole way. I kept several cars behind and tried to be in a different lane whenever possible. After an hour, he signalled left and we both exited the motorway.

We remained on dual carriageways for about ten minutes before the roads became more suburban and pedestrianised. Finally, he turned into a cul-de-sac filled with large houses with an abundance of foliage. I waited at the end of the road for what felt like an eternity, but was only about five minutes, then slowly drove up the street. I was looking out for the car but had no intention of stopping. When I saw the silver Merc parked up, with Colin walking towards the door, I knew my mission was accomplished. I stopped at the end of the road and made a quick note of the address, and dropped a pin on my sat nav app so I knew where to find it. I then turned around and drove all the way home with my thinking cap on, ready to plan the next phase of this investigation – the stakeout.

There are two kinds of stakeout – the kind where so much activity is happening that one has to have laser focus to not be distracted, and the kind where almost nothing happens at all right until you're about to give up.

This stakeout was the latter.

LEADS FOR LEADS

I parked the inconspicuous black Ford Focus (that I borrowed from my friend Trudy to add an extra layer of anonymity) at the top of Milton Grove – the small cul-de-sac that I had followed Colin to the week prior. I'd taken a stroll around the street several times in the days leading up to my surveillance with my dog Barry, to get the lay of the land and to find the best vantage point for my survey. At the top of the grove was a small, public car park – it seemed out of place at first but then I realised it was adjacent to an alleyway that led to a parade of shops. I made sure there were no parking restrictions – none after 6pm thankfully – and chose a space right in the corner. I had a clear view of a large house and the four small stone steps that led up to it. I could also see the houses on both sides, the roads into the cul-de-sac and the alleyway to the shops. It was the perfect spot, near enough to a lamp post to light the inside of my car, but not so near that it shone a spotlight on me.

I've discovered, after years of being asked the same questions when people find out I am a PI, that no one really understands the intensity of surveillance. Quite a lot of training is required to be able to stay focused and alert for long periods of time. I can't be distracted by reading a book or looking at my phone; all I can do is watch. I pass the time with music, audiobooks or podcasts. Things that can keep my mind going but don't take my eyes away from the subject.

I'm also always asked what I do about needing the

toilet. That's something that also took some training – to put it simply, I don't. I limit how much water or tea I drink before and during the surveillance to ensure it's not interrupted by nature calling. It's one of the more difficult aspects, but, after many long surveillance sessions, I've trained my body and mind to overcome it.

The plan for this particular evening was to sit here for a few hours to wait for Colin's arrival. Jeanette had checked his phone's location earlier that day and it showed him at his office. When she checked it again as it neared 5pm, the tracking was off. That was the pattern I had observed, so it was safe to assume he was on his way to Milton Grove. After confirming his arrival, I planned to wait a while to see how long he stayed.

From leaving his office at approximately 5pm, it should take Colin about two and a half hours to get to where I knew he parked the car. To be safe, I arrived at six, after checking the traffic to see that it was moderate but not too heavy, typical for a Friday night, so my timings should be accurate.

It was October, so the sun was well on its way to bed when I arrived; and it would be almost pitch black by 7pm, so, on the very off chance Colin happened to park near me, he wouldn't see me.

I kept a watchful eye on the street from the moment I arrived, only breaking eye contact with the house to check my notes. I was looking out for the same silver Mercedes that I had observed him driving on the first evening of surveillance. For extra vigilance, I noted down every car that came down the street. It was a quiet cul-de-sac, so I didn't expect to see many.

> Red Mini Cooper, white Renault van, light green Fiat 500, black BMW, silver Ford Transit van. Three couples walking dogs of various sizes and breeds — my eyes aren't what they used to be so forgive me for not knowing exactly what they were!
> Small gathering of teenagers going through the alleyway, then returning ten minutes later with a pizza box.

It was getting close to 7pm, so I put down the notebook and watched closely, with one hand on my long-lens camera, poised and ready to grab the evidence.

7:15 rolled past, then 7:30 . . . then finally, just as I started to think tonight was not the night, at 7:42 the headlights of a silver Mercedes C class – Colin's to be exact – grabbed my attention and illuminated the street as it turned the corner.

'Gotcha!' I said to myself, doing a small happy wiggle in my seat. I grabbed my camera and took a few photographs of the car approaching the house with the four stone steps. It stopped right outside, and idled for a few minutes. After what felt like an eternity, the engine turned off and the door opened.

Just then my phone beeped – it was set to 'do not disturb', so would only allow emergency calls or messages, and communication from Jeanette. I darted my eyes to it quickly to see Jeanette saying,

> He's just texted me, the bastard! Said he's just got home and going to bed! Pleeeeaaase tell me you've got him!

I waited until I knew for sure it was him before taking any more photos. Then Colin's six-foot frame gracefully stepped from the car. He was looking pleased with himself. I snapped a few more photos, capturing him from his car all the way to the front door, where he was greeted by a tall, voluptuous beauty with copper hair, dressed in – what appeared to be – nothing but a robe.

'Ugh, such a cliché!' I said to myself, aghast.

There could still be a reasonable explanation for him being at this place, which definitely wasn't his home. I couldn't think of anything that would make this seem innocuous, but cheaters are the best liars, so I needed more evidence.

I stayed until 11pm. There was no further activity on the street, apart from a delivery service arriving at the house at approximately 9pm. Ms Copper answered the door – slightly more clothed – but I hadn't seen Colin leave, so it was clear it was for both of them and that he'd probably be here for the night now.

By this point I was tired to the bone – it's strangely exhausting just sitting and watching. So I started the car and headed off to the hotel two miles up the road where I had booked a room just in case.

By the time I got to my room the hotel bar and restaurant had closed, so, taking inspiration from Ms Copper, I ordered some Chinese food. I wolfed it down as soon as it arrived, then promptly crashed out – though not before setting my alarm for 6am. I still had a cheater to catch, after all.

I only managed about an hour of sleep due to the anticipation of the following morning's investigation (and perhaps a little bit from eating so late). By the time my 6am alarm went off, I was up, showered, dressed in my finest dog-walking clothes (stained leggings, a fleece jumper and a beanie hat) and caffeinated. I popped my room key in the checkout box, jumped in the car, and drove back to Milton Grove to execute the final phase of the plan to catch Colin.

This time, I parked round the corner, about 200 yards away from the entrance to the cul-de-sac. I would do the rest on foot.

I opened my boot and slung on a tatty coat with a few strands of dog hair on – intentionally added by letting Barry kip on my coat a few days prior. I then grabbed a battered old dog lead and a handful of dog biscuits to stuff into my pocket. I walked the opposite direction, towards a small patch of greenery near the shops, then through the alleyway on to Milton Grove.

Putting on my best distressed look, I pretended to search. I looked under cars, peered over fences, and called, 'Here boy' in a high-pitched voice that started to annoy even myself after a while.

To anyone who knew me, I'd looked like I'd lost my mind. But to people on Milton Grove, I looked like I'd lost my dog – and that was how I would get the attention of Ms Copper and Colin.

My head flew up as if I had heard something as I approached the house with the four stone steps. I wasn't sure if the inhabitants could see me but to be safe I had to remain staunchly in character. I walked up the steps, continuing to search in the bushes, until I reached the doorbell and rang it.

Ms Copper opened the door. 'Can I help you?' she asked politely.

'I'm terribly sorry to bother you so early, I live round the corner and was out for a walk on the green with my dog but he slipped his lead and I can't find him,' I told her, holding up the empty lead as though it was evidence. 'I'm sure I heard his bark coming from this way, so I wondered if you could check your back garden for me?'

Ms Copper seemed genuinely upset for me, and I was secretly pleased that my ruse was so convincing.

'Colin, darling, could you come here for a moment?' she called back into the house.

And there he was, coming down the stairs in low-hanging pyjama trousers and a vest, looking as if he'd just woken up.

'Oh, hello,' he said, clocking me at the door, 'Honey, who's this, is everything okay?' he asked Ms Copper.

'Yes, this poor lady – sorry, what was your name?'

'Jenny,' I told her, intentionally using a name that sounded like Colin's wife's name.

'Jenny is a neighbour and her poor dog has run away. She was hoping we could check our garden. Would you pop out and have a look?' she asked him.

I noticed how she said *our* garden, leaving a mental note to come back to that later.

'Urm, yeah, sure – what does he look like?' he asked and I couldn't help but think it was a silly question. If there was *any* dog in the garden, it would be that one. But the question gave me an opportunity to reach for my phone.

'Ah, yes of course, let me just find a photo.' I reached my hand into my right-hand pocket and thumbed over the devices held there, careful not to pull out the Dictaphone that had been recording since I rang the doorbell.

With a bit of sleight of hand, and a 'come on, bloody technology' comment, I set a three-minute timer and took a series of photos with my phone showing Colin in his state of undress, Ms Copper and the entryway to the home, before opening up a photo of Barry to show him. He padded off to the garden, grabbing some slippers on his way.

While he was gone, Ms Copper – Abbie, she told me – said she thought she'd seen me walking my dog around here recently and he seemed like a 'nice boy' and she hoped he showed up soon. I was pleased that my dog walks in the area gave me an extra layer of credibility.

'I really appreciate your husband checking for me,' I told Abbie.

'Oh no Colin isn't my husband, just my boyfriend – but hey, maybe one day!' She let out a small, innocent giggle.

'Ah I see, sorry. This is a lovely home, do you both live here?' I asked, trying to figure out just how serious this relationship was and how much Abbie knew about Colin's life. It was unlikely she'd mention his wife even if she knew, but she might accidentally give something away. I noticed Colin wasn't wearing a wedding ring; paired with Abbie's 'one day' comment, this made me fairly sure she had no clue.

'Unfortunately not. Colin works quite far away, so he has his own place near work, but comes here as often as he can.'

As he returned, he looked apologetic and – unsurprisingly – told me there was no dog to be found.

The timer went off just as planned, and I 'answered' the pretend call, stepping back a bit so they couldn't tell that I was speaking to nobody. I let out a huge sigh and said, 'Oh thank goodness!' to the imaginary person on the other end of the phone. I turned to Abbie with a big, relieved grin and declared, 'I'm so sorry to have disturbed you, he's been found on the other side of the street – my number is on the collar, and a kind gentleman has hold of him, so I better dash! Have a lovely day.' Then I hurried back down the four stone steps, hearing Abbie shouting, 'Nice to meet you, I'm so glad you've found him.' I skipped back to my car, only reaching into my pocket to turn off the Dictaphone when I was out of sight.

I checked the images I had captured on my phone. It was a risky move, as the entire set-up would have been a waste of time if I didn't capture the footage correctly, but thankfully the images were clear as day and exactly what Jeanette needed to prove her husband was cheating.

I began typing a message to Jeanette to tell her I would be in touch when I got home in a few hours, but I realised that would just leave her hanging even longer, so I decided against it and decided to get home, write up my notes and prepare an evidence document to show her the whole picture.

And with that, I hit the road.

'I knew it! I bloody knew it!' Jeanette stood up with fire in her eyes when I told her I had proof of Colin's infidelity.

We met up in the same coffee shop near where she lived so I could present her with the docket of information I had gathered. I showed her everything, leading with the photos.

'Oh my god I know her! She was a temp at his office about a year ago, I saw her a few times whenever our paths crossed with work. It was rare, and Colin and I never worked together, but once or twice a year we'd have meetings there and I remember her – Annie? Something like that. Bloody cliché!'

She was enraged. I didn't correct her with Abbie's real name, she'd hear it on the recording anyway.

'Did she know you two are married?' I asked, tentatively, as at this point I was quite sure she didn't and I'd be a bit miffed with myself for reading that wrong.

'I didn't tell her – we kept things separate at work, and I didn't think she even knew Colin. What a pig that man is.'

I stifled a small laugh; it's not my place to engage like that, but I couldn't help finding Jeanette's comments amusing.

'So, million-pound question: what are you going to do next?' I asked.

'Divorce him.'

That was case closed on Jeanette and Colin, but Jeanette and I kept in touch and she kept me up to date with the situation with Colin.

About a year or so later, she was happily divorced. By the time she filed, the laws had changed and adultery was no longer a recognised reason, so it was down as 'The Irretrievable Breakdown of the Marriage', but, as far as Jeanette – or anybody who asked – was concerned, it was purely down to his adultery.

'I don't know if we'd have made it, anyway,' she told me when we met for a drink after the divorce was finalised. 'Living apart seemed like it worked for us, but maybe it didn't. Or it did for him, as he was able to hide an affair!'

Jeanette is now in a long-term relationship with someone else; he's already asked her to move in with him. She's holding up her stubborn ways about having her own house, but she's coming round to the idea of him moving in there. She seems genuinely very happy – a far cry from the rage-fuelled Jeanette I'd met not too long ago.

As far as I know, Colin and Abbie's relationship is still going, but Jeanette wanted Abbie to have all the facts, and managed to get in touch with her to tell her he was married when their relationship started. A conversation she revelled in.

PI Perspective

I've said it before and I'll say it until I am blue in the face. Cheaters are clever. But I am cleverer. It might take a dog lead, a few goes up and down the M4 and a stakeout to catch them in the act, but I will.

Although, realistically, I wouldn't classify Colin's behaviour as merely cheating. This was much more than that, and simply calling him a cheater doesn't do it justice. There should be a stronger word. I mean, I can think of a few with four letters, but most are not appropriate for everyday use.

What shocks me most is that Colin appeared to have an entire life outside of his marriage. While I knew their living situation was unconventional, Jeanette had told me that it had worked for them for so long, and I had done my best to understand. It felt like a bigger slap in the face to Jeanette that he was not only carrying on with someone else, but it seemed that the same live-apart relationship was happening in full with another person. This wasn't just casual; they seemed to have built a life together.

I also felt sad for Abbie. If she truly didn't know about Jeanette – I'd have no proof either way, but my gut told me she was in the dark – she was another innocent person dragged into the selfish greed and audacity of a man who wanted to have his cake and eat it.

The biggest takeaway from Jeanette's case is that regardless of the circumstances, cheaters often behave the same way. Severe emotional and behavioural shifts are the biggest clues that something is amiss, which is exactly what tipped Jeanette off and made her suspicious of Colin. That's not to say that all changes equal cheating; they're just often a precursor to other signs such as changing phone or tablet passwords, a sudden interest in their own appearance, unexplained expenses, changes in intimacy and lack of interest in their partner.

These behaviours are not proof alone, but they're enough to raise suspicion and force the sceptical person to look for answers. I always trust my own gut; if you suspect a cheater, I implore you to trust yours.

CHAPTER 4

The Case That Wasn't

If I Hadn't Trusted My Gut, Would She Be Dead Now?

Intuition. It's one of the most important skills for an investigator, and one that I have learned to rely on. It's a critical part of my process and, in this particular case, a life depended on it.

There's a huge gulf between instinct and intuition. Instinct is covering your face when you sense an object hurtling towards it; it is something we all have, something we are born with, something critical to our survival. But intuition is different. It's that gut feeling or a gnawing sensation you have when something isn't quite right. It's not trusting someone but not really knowing why. It's a feeling that you can't quite shake but know you should trust – and it's what made this case particularly interesting, because if I hadn't trusted my intuition a woman could have been killed.

My laptop dinged unexpectedly. It was 8:45pm and I was finishing up a report, ready to wind down for the night. My dog was desperately craving my presence on the sofa, my husband too. I considered leaving it until tomorrow, but often cases are time-critical and I pride myself on being available should someone need me – even during *The Great British Bake Off*.

The message came through via Facebook.

> Dear Alison, I hope you are able to help me. I didn't think people actually hired PIs but here we go . . . My fiancée, Alice, has gone missing and I need your help to find her, before it's too late

Jack went on to give me some more details about his relationship with Alice, and why he was so concerned about her leaving. He referred to her as 'missing' but I hesitate to use that particular word, loaded as it is.

Did you know that legally any person can 'go missing' of their own accord at any time? The reasons for which people go missing are broad and varied, for example someone could simply move away without informing anyone – something they are legally entitled to do. This doesn't necessarily qualify them as a missing person. With Jack and Alice, it seemed to be a simple case of one partner choosing to leave and the other not being quite ready to accept that – at least that was how Jack portrayed it.

Jack told me more about his relationship with Alice and that they had been together for many years, and now they were engaged. According to Jack they were blissfully happy, planning their wedding, until one day Alice up and left.

'I didn't understand how she was feeling and I think I handled it incorrectly, which pushed her away.'

I try to remain neutral with all my cases – to do otherwise, to be drawn in, can cloud one's judgement. But in this instance, I must confess, Jack's story moved me. Perhaps it was the thought that a loved one, someone with whom you have mapped out one long future, could extinguish those plans in an instant. Or perhaps it was the thought that we never really know the people who sleep beside us. Whatever the reason, I could tell he was hurting and I knew I would be able to help, so I agreed to meet to discuss his case.

Safety is important. I make a point of meeting potential clients in a public place, but discreet enough for them to be able to talk freely. Jack lived in a suburb just outside of North London, so I journeyed down from my home in Oxford to meet him at a coffee shop. I grabbed a cup of tea and sat down at a table near the back. I was a bit early, so I had another read through the messages between us and the questions I had prepared.

A short while later the door pinged and in walked an almost-six-foot man, dressed in dark denim jeans and a peach-coloured polo shirt. I immediately recognised him from his profile picture. He shook my hand, introduced himself as Jack and offered to buy me a drink. I am never one to say no to a cuppa. He shortly returned with my tea, a coffee for himself and some biscuits he said were for us to share. Immediately I was impressed with how polite and well-put-together he seemed, but, from the dark circles that clung to the recesses of his lower eyelids, I could tell he was rattled; in desperate need of a good night's sleep, and closure.

He was passionate when he told me that Alice had walked out on him two weeks ago, explaining that she was unhappy in the relationship and that it wasn't going to work out. She left and Jack had not heard from her since, which, even though they had separated, was unlike her. While he found the break-up difficult to comprehend, he knew Alice well enough to know there was no changing her mind, and he accepted the fact that his relationship was over.

'I don't think she's ever coming back,' Jack said, eyes glassy with emotion. His voice wobbled as he told me about the argument they had before she left. 'It was just one of those stupid fights that couples have. At first I thought she just needed to cool off but she said it was over and that I had to leave her alone.

'Of course, I want to respect her wishes and give her the space she needs, I just need to know she is okay.' He took a deep breath and I noticed his eyes briefly darting to the left as his fingers tapped against the side of his coffee mug. 'But, also . . .' He stuttered and took a pause, during which my PI senses started tingling. There's always a *but also.*

He further explained that, while he was concerned for her welfare, perhaps more importantly he wanted help retrieving his grandmother's ring, which he gave Alice when he proposed. The ring was a family heirloom and it meant the world to him and his family.

Jack leaned forward on the cafe table, his chin resting on his cupped hands.

'I still remember the look on her face when I proposed. She knew the ring existed and how special it was to my family, so she seemed genuinely gobsmacked that I was giving it to her.' He smiled, as he reminisced about getting down on one knee.

'I'm hurt that she left, but I'm equally hurt that she took something so important. It's like she broke my heart twice,' he continued. It was clear that the emotional attachment Jack felt went beyond his love for Alice. He seemed to mourn his future with her and was desperately sad about her taking the ring – sadness, with a hint of anger.

We talked at length about why he had reached out to a private investigator and not the police, seeing as such a priceless piece of jewellery was involved. He explained he wanted to settle this civilly; involving the police was a last resort. Jack chose me to help him, he said, as he felt Alice would respond better to a female approach. I get this a lot, and it's what, I think, gives me an edge. There are very few women in my line of work.

While the field is male-dominated (how I loathe that term) the number of female private investigators is slowly increasing. Women can bring valuable skills and perspectives through our lived experiences that our male counterparts cannot.

The 'man's world' archetype is mostly to blame – investigations are seen as confrontational and possibly dangerous, not appropriate for women to be involved with. Concerns of safety and physical risk can be high, but in reality, most investigations involve a lot of sitting around and quick thinking. As I've said before, there's very little of the fighting and car chases depicted in the media.

Only once has my safety come into question, and that turned out to be nothing anyway. I was once noticed by the neighbour of one of my subjects, and after a luke-warm exchange through my car door window, he left me alone.

Jack talked and talked about his life with Alice, and I listened, carefully, and encouraged him to open up to me, bit by bit. In doing so, I couldn't help but observe some inconsistencies in his story. Throughout our correspondence and meeting, he told me they'd been together 'many years' or 'a long time', but there was never a date to anything. But the further he delved into their relationship, the more specific he started to get. He proposed on their two-year anniversary, which, coincidentally, was also Valentine's Day. Later on he mentioned they met in

April – so they started dating before they met. Perhaps they were friends for a while and they got together the following year, but then those dates didn't line up either. Maybe Jack misspoke, or maybe Jack was lying.

We chatted for some time. I like to learn as much as I can about both client and subject. The more information I have, the clearer the picture of their life together, and the better the assumptions I can make. In many ways it's like completing a jigsaw. You start with the corners, the edges, look for the pieces that share similarities, and then gradually work your way to the middle, filling in the blanks. You can interpret a lot just by talking to someone – a flick of a wrist, a rub of the eye, an unexpected inflection at the end of a statement. I learned a lot from what he said, and a lot more from what he didn't.

Among the glamorous dates and luxury holidays, the perfect home and the pretty posed photographs, something was missing. The warmth of his impassioned speech about her leaving turned cold when speaking about when they were happy. Perhaps this was the heartbreak talking, maybe he found it too difficult to be heartfelt. I couldn't be sure. But I kept that thought in the back of my mind – I would need it later.

We spent the better part of the afternoon together – a further cup of tea and a cheese toastie later, I still wasn't sure what to do. The alarm bells of intuition were ringing loudly in my head as I drifted between feeling sorry for Jack and being wary of him. He was very likeable, charming, and seemingly good-natured, but I just couldn't quash the heavy disquiet in the pit of my stomach.

On the train home I picked at an overpriced chicken salad sandwich as I replayed the conversation over and over again in my head. There was definitely a mystery here, I just wasn't quite sure if it was as Jack had presented it. My mind had begun to wander when a Facebook message pinged me from my daydream. It was Jack, already chasing answers. Then followed the consent letter I had asked him for this afternoon – a legal requirement when looking to recover someone's property. In the letter he stated that he granted me permission to look for his item and granted me temporary custody should it be recovered. He also included a photo of the ring: a large sapphire set in a white gold claw, with two small diamonds either side, and a white gold band. It was beautiful and distinctive; you would definitely notice it – especially notice it missing. I could see why someone would want it back.

I couldn't explain why, but his overeagerness and marked impatience amplified my concerns. I shot a message back to Jack saying that I had more due-diligence to complete before I would formally accept the case. I forewarned him that this could involve a bit of background research, which he consented to – 'anything to help me find her,' he said. Something just didn't feel right and I needed some time to process. Yes, I was potentially saying goodbye to a rather sizable payday, but no sum could make me cast aside my integrity or – as I would later discover

– ignore someone in danger of violence, or worse. Had I known then what I know now, I'd have been straight to the police station to hand over Jack's details.

Finding Alice

During our meeting, Jack had explained that Alice didn't take much with her – certainly not enough to start a whole new life, he said, but enough to conclude that she was gone for good. He had pointed out that her passport was gone, as well as some of her most treasured items. Including, of course, the ring.

He told me stories of her past conduct, how it was concerning for him and how she could return to that pattern. Most of these stories involved travel and, with her passport missing, it would be safe to assume she was abroad. So my first step was to establish a pattern of behaviour.

Has she done this before? Does she tend to travel, if so, where and how? Does she have family or friends overseas that Jack didn't know about? These were just some of the questions darting through my mind as I sat in my office, with Barry snoring softly, nestled by my slippered feet.

My first port of call was to check the missing persons databases. Surely Jack couldn't be the only one looking for her if Alice was truly 'missing'. But Jack's clear lack of interest in involving the police led me to believe the database wouldn't have the answer. I was correct. As a private investigator, it's better this way. Without intervention from the police I could investigate freely, albeit off the record.

While Jack had given a detailed description of Alice and their relationship, there were still a lot of gaps for me to piece together to build an accurate picture of their life together. As she was in her late twenties, I went to the first place I knew would prove a treasure trove of intel: her social media.

'Ok, Alice Kent,' I muttered to myself, 'who are you?' Social media sites such as Facebook, X (formerly Twitter) and Instagram have given never-before-seen visibility to a person's life and activities. Checking in, posting photos, liking pages and updating statuses have seemingly become an essential part of our day-to-day lives. With smartphones, we're constantly logged in (or can be at the touch of a button) to a completely public platform – for better or for worse. As a mother, I loathe social media. My daughter's teenage years coincided with the rise of these ubiquitous platforms, much to my and my husband's dismay. Secret-keeping and covert plans with friends were made significantly easier when they could be hidden away in a pocket. However, as a private investigator, social media is my dearest friend – albeit one you only really spend time with when you want something.

Social media investigations can bring to light a great deal of information about a person. It's very common for people to reveal things about themselves completely unintentionally, and I've spent years studying and analysing online behaviour to help better understand people I otherwise might not be able to meet.

THE CASE THAT WASN'T

I found Alice's Facebook profile – sometimes this lead can fall flat, as a lot of people set their profiles to private, but fortunately Alice's was public, so I could see almost everything. I skimmed through her latest check-ins and posts and there had been nothing new since a few days before Jack said she left. However, I could discern that she *had* been online, and, interestingly, her relationship status was hidden. Now this could have always been this way, but in my experience people are often not ready to set it to 'single' but do not want their relationship to be public knowledge, so they hide this information. Unfortunately, there is no way to be sure either way.

Her activity and check-ins were sporadic, which made it difficult to form an idea of her typical comings and goings, but, reading between the lines, much could be gleaned. Judging from the check-ins she was tagged in, she went out with a friend every two to three weeks. Most likely she went out alone more but didn't share it on social media. I noted that none of the posts about her movements were her own; they were all things she had been tagged in. Did this mean she was very private? Or perhaps just didn't use Facebook that much?

Her tags told me that they liked to try new places and activities. Sometimes they'd stay local; mostly coffee shops, shopping centres and bookshops within a few miles of the area in which she lived. But if they were looking for a bar or some live music, then central London was the place she'd be.

I took a break from the screen, pushing away from my desk and taking off my red-rimmed glasses. I sighed, realising I hadn't seen a single mention of Jack on her Facebook yet. I got up and strode into the kitchen to pop the kettle on. Mark joined me, silently taking over, delicately pointing me towards the table. He's a detective, of sorts, in his own right; he's fantastic at telling when there's something bugging me, and even better at knowing when to ask – this was definitely not the time.

The uncertain feeling I'd had as I finished my meeting with Jack was still there – in fact it had redoubled. *Something with this story just isn't right*, I thought, as I chewed the inside of my cheek.

Deciding to avoid my office for the rest of the day, I grabbed my tea and a handful of grapes and sat on the patio in the back garden. A cold wind was rattling through me, but the fresh air was helping to gently untie the knot in my stomach, one fibril at a time.

I perched my laptop on the garden table, took a huge gulp of tea, and began my next steps to find Alice.

Her Facebook photos were rather conveniently sorted into albums, which was spectacularly useful when trying to discern if there were particular places she liked to visit. I looked through *Greece 2014*, *Turkey 2016* and *Ibiza 2018*, finding no particular trends to follow there. Though I couldn't help but notice a lot of selfies, memes, food and scenery photos. Only her tagged photos involved other people, and still nothing of Jack. Could she have deleted them? Or did they not exist?

At this point I truly believed they had a genuine relationship; even the best liar couldn't feign that much passion. I can spot a lie from a mile off – it's been one of my greatest gifts, and one that has found its natural (and most useful) expression in my career to date. I believed the relationship existed. I believed Jack's feelings were real – but were Alice's? Did she feel the same way? Or was she going along with a fiction that she hoped, one day, she herself would buy into?

Many of her photos were shared to Facebook via Instagram, showing me she favoured image-based communication. There, I decided, would be where I'd likely find more information.

I'll admit, I'm not hugely au fait with Instagram. I roughly know my way around – enough to find out what I need. But it's not as straightforward as it is with Facebook. Users have their own unique username, not strictly related to their actual name. That doesn't mean I *can't* find people, though . . .

I hit a few wrong turns, but eventually I struck gold. I found Alice's profile and looked through her images. They were mostly the same groups and locations, but there were a few more with other people involved – you could tell these were her images due to the poses and camera position. I cross-checked the friends with the ones on Facebook and found no inconsistencies, meaning I hadn't found some elusive new person who could shed some light on this. Crucially, I had still yet to unearth any photos of Jack.

Scrolling back and forth between her pictures, I noticed that about eight months ago her posting pattern changed. Previously she had posted quite regularly, showing an active social life (wildly different to her Facebook presence). I smiled as I scrolled through photos of her and her friends going to restaurants, dancing at clubs, clinking glasses at birthday parties and New Year's celebrations. There were day trips and mini breaks, even some sports and a hiking trip – things about Alice that Jack hadn't mentioned. Then suddenly everything slowed down, and in those few months she only posted a handful of images, including some random scenery captured through what appeared to be a train or car window, a glass of wine on a dinner table, a dog that the caption informed me was her neighbour's, and other inconsequential images with brief, or non-existent, captions. No fun nights out, no trips. It was like something happened earlier in the year that made her change drastically, that made her become someone else.

The sun began to set and a chill hit the air. The smell of dinner wafted out of the kitchen and I knew it was time to call it a day, so I yet again closed the lid of my laptop and walked back inside, giving Barry a delicate pat on the way past, before extending the same courtesy to Mark.

An investigation often starts like this. You can look and look but not really find what it is you need. The answers so rarely jump out at you. It takes time, patience, and a mind that is always turning details over, examining them – the edges, the corners, the seemingly inconsequential – until a detail will snag, like a hangnail catching on a loose fibre in a threadbare jacket.

I tucked into my dinner that night with a glass of red while I tried to take my mind off Jack and Alice.

Then it dawned on me. Literally. I woke up first thing and immediately thought of all those photos, events, celebrations and happy times. But where was the ring? I grabbed my phone, leaving a snoring Mark and allowing Barry to hop into my spot as I hotfooted it to the kitchen to put the kettle on.

Jack told me they got engaged in the summer over a year ago, so there should be at least a few months in which she was wearing the ring in those photos. She had posted lots during that time but there were absolutely no signs of the big blue stone that Jack was so desperate for me to retrieve.

Nothing was adding up, and something deep down told me that this relationship was not at all as Jack portrayed it. The seeds of doubt had grown into a forest.

Back to Jack

You can tell so much about a person from their body language and how they talk, so I decided I needed to see Jack again to understand this case a bit better. But this time my guard would be up even higher. If this was a legitimate case, he (to some extent) deserved my benefit of the doubt and I should at least fill him in on what I thought so far. My thoughts at this point were still just an educated guess, after all.

'Hello?' answered a groggy-sounding Jack.

'Hi Jack, sorry for the early call but I hoped we could meet today. I just want to ask a few more questions to help me find Alice.'

I kept it vague, I didn't want him to think I had any suspicions about him.

'Urm . . . yeah, okay. Same place at ten.'

I agreed and hung up the phone, then raced to the shower to get ready, as I wanted to be there before him; it's a bit of a power play to arrive first, and helps me feel more in control. Once I got to the café, I tucked myself in a corner, slightly out of view from the door so I could see him as he came in but he couldn't see me. I wanted to observe him being natural and to see if the emotional guy I had met before was the act that I assumed it was. If his emotional demeanour was just a facade. It seems like such a small trick, but this simple act reveals so much about a person.

He arrived in a suit, looking much more together than the first time we met. He seemed more confident and controlled, with no trace of emotion on his face as he strolled into the cafe. He was scanning the room, his eyes darting around but barely moving his body. He reminded me of a scene in *The Terminator*, where Schwarzenegger moves through the bar searching around, seemingly oblivious to everyone else; just stoic, in search of his target. To be honest, he gave me the creeps. He stood tall, like he owned the place, and I immediately felt intimidated, until I reminded myself that I had the upper hand. I watched him for another thirty seconds or so before I gave him a wave as if I had only just seen him. He immediately put his mask back on and the heartbroken, friendly Jack appeared – it would have been impressive if it wasn't so infuriating. The gnawing feeling that this man was not telling the truth was eating me up, and with every move he made I felt more and more certain that this case was based on a lie. His eyes and shoulders stooped simultaneously as he slumped over to me.

'Ali, it's nice to see you again.' He sighed.

'Thanks for meeting me today, Jack. You look like you're off somewhere important, I hope I'm not keeping you.'

'No, I just popped out of work, this is much, much more important. Have you any news on my love?'

His tone was pointed, like he was really trying to make me believe him. The way he phrased it almost made me dry-heave. It felt so false and an unnecessary way to ask me about Alice. He hadn't used language like that before, often only referring to her as 'my fiancée' or by her name. It was unsettling. I didn't want him to know that I suspected he was lying about something. I needed him to believe that I was completely on his side so I could catch him in a lie.

'Well, the strange thing is, I've discovered Alice's social

media and it looks like she's been living a totally different life online to what you've told me.' I explained that there was no mention of him on her socials, nor any reference to any of the trips or experiences they had shared. Images that appeared to be from her home were not as described by Jack. She seemed like an entirely different person.

'She thought of herself as an "influencer".' His hands making air-quotes as he said the word with distain. 'She wanted to have a huge social media following and apparently that is more lucrative if you appear single. She didn't share her *real* life on social, just something fabricated for clicks.'

'Oh . . . I see. That seems like something you should have mentioned earlier on as you knew checking her socials was going to be a huge part of this investigation.'

'I was embarrassed,' he blurted out. He didn't seem embarrassed; just frustrated at this line of questioning. 'You see, she was a bit of a . . . well, a mess at times.'

He had touched on this before, so I encouraged him to elaborate.

He explained that Alice regularly got herself into situations where she needed large sums of money, and theorised that this was the reason she took the ring. He told me stories about her drinking to excess and on one occasion falling asleep on a train only to end up on the other side of London, leaving Jack to pick up a hefty taxi bill.

'She went to America with some friends in the summer,' he explained sounding frustrated, 'and called me asking for bail money as she'd got herself arrested! What an embarrassment!' His nostrils flared, but I didn't quite buy this one. I couldn't tell if he was frustrated with my questioning, or frustrated about the story. Neither really painted him in the best light.

'Summer of which year?'

'Last year.'

'When you got engaged? Before or after?'

His right knuckles whitened as his grip became more intense – he could tell I had caught him in a lie. I wasn't sure if the trip or the engagement was the lie, so I would need to probe a bit deeper to get to the bottom of this one. His body language was as if he was ready to just blurt it all out but he knew he couldn't, so he focused all that energy into his joints. His whole body was tense and his eyes darted around. Perhaps he was desperately looking for his next lie. To the untrained eye this could look like he was upset by my findings, but I knew better.

As quickly as it came, the strain left his face and his steely eyes fixed on a position behind my head. It happened so fast I actually turned to see what he was looking at – but he was looking right through me.

'Before . . .' He must have noticed my eyebrow rise; he quickly added, 'But I was so overcome with love for her, and the fear that she could have been hurt, I still went ahead with my proposal. Even with the problems, I couldn't be without her . . . that's why I'm in so much pain now.' He leaned forward with his forehead on his hand, as if trying to show me his devastation. But it was too late. The spell had been broken and I could no longer believe a single word he said – not that I had for a while anyway.

'I think I have all I need now,' I told him, rising to my feet. 'I'll be in touch.' I left the cafe quickly, giving my intuition an imaginary high-five for seeing me right yet again. Of course, I still didn't know anything for certain, and I definitely didn't know quite how sinister Jack was. I headed home, planning my next steps.

As I arrived back at Oxford station, I still didn't know what to do. At this point I still hadn't formally accepted the case, despite hours of work on it. I knew for sure I didn't feel comfortable helping Jack. I am good at finding the truth, but when lies pile up on other lies, it's hard to see the wood for the trees. It was so frustrating and I knew I had to make a decision.

When I arrived home, I went straight into my office and grabbed a notepad from my shelf. I have at least ten notepads of varying sizes and styles and I subconsciously pick the one that matches my mood. The grey A5 pad was completely new and I had a brief moment of reprieve as I opened it and cracked the spine; running my hands along the fresh pages. 'If all else fails,' I tell myself, 'write a list.'

Writing PROS and CONS at the top of the page, I used a ruler and red pen to split the page in two. Under PROS were 'if I find Alice I can help her' and '£££' (which is never the reason to take a case, but I couldn't think of any other good reason). The CONS list was longer: 'Jack gives me the creeps', 'Jack is lying about something' and 'seems like Alice doesn't want to be found'.

I tore the paper out of my notebook, screwed it up, and launched it towards the small bin on the other side of my desk. As it bounced off the rim, a message appeared in my inbox from Jack. I assumed he wanted an update – it had only been a few hours, but he didn't know how long it takes me to get home.

Too late, I've got someone else now.

I felt a small rush of relief, but that quickly turned into panic. I did not trust Jack, but someone else had – was this going to put Alice in danger? I didn't know what to do, yet again. It's a feeling I am not used to, and I do not like it. Usually never one to clock off early, I uncharacteristically shut my laptop and walked away.

Finally, Some Answers

Days had passed and I buried myself in other cases to get Jack and Alice out of my mind. I hate leaving a case unsolved but I felt it would be immoral and irresponsible to carry on. Occasionally I thought about how if I'd have just said yes at the beginning, I'd have been quids in, but my standards are far more important to me than a payday. But what *had* happened to Alice? It made me feel on edge all the time. I thought about raising the issue with the police, but I had no evidence whatsoever, and what I felt was not probable cause.

I was pulled away from the sinking, sick feeling in my gut by the sound of my phone ringing from the other room. Mark answered and very timidly popped his head into my office.

'I'm just wrapping up this insurance fraud case, I'll be out in a mo,' I called without turning my head.

'Ali . . . ?' Mark's tone immediately got my attention and I spun my chair round, almost giving myself vertigo.

'The police want to speak to you,' he told me. 'They'd like you to go in and make a statement.'

In my gut, I knew this was about Jack.

A boldly spoken man, who introduced himself as Officer Dixon, greeted me at the station entrance, and shook my hand vigorously. I could feel the sweat from my anxious palm squish into his, which made my entire body tense up. I felt strangely nervous, like I had done something wrong, as at this point I didn't actually know for sure what had happened. I was summoned with no information whatsoever and I, yet again, found myself completely at a loss.

Assuming this was about Jack, I had brought my case notes with me, tucked into my large black handbag. I held it close to my body as if guarding national secrets.

Dixon walked me along the corridor and opened a door marked 'Interview Room 2'. The room was bleak and smelt like a repulsive mix of stale coffee and old shoes. Like a high school PE changing room. The walls looked like they were once white, but years of sweaty suspects and tension had turned them beige and dirty. I was directed to a small metal desk in the centre of the room and asked to sit in an uncomfortable chair. I felt like a criminal, but reminded myself that I had done nothing wrong.

'Thanks for coming in, Ms Marsh.'

'Ali, please.'

'Noted. Ali, this is Officer Lupton, who will be joining us today.' He gestured to a young officer standing coyly in the corner. 'Just to preface this, you're not in any trouble, but could you please describe how you know Mr Jack Cann?' Officer Dixon asked as he sat down opposite me in an equally uncomfortable-looking chair. I let out a long, loud sigh – partly out of relief but mostly to steel myself ready for whatever was coming next. I quickly learned that nothing could have prepared me for what Officers Dixon and Lupton had to say.

I learned that officers had found my website, emails and phone number on Jack's phone and computer, so my input on their investigation was of high interest.

What investigation? I thought to myself. I still had no clue. I knew he seemed like an absolute toerag, but was he actually a criminal?

'We're particularly interested in what Mr Cann told you about Miss Kent, and what you know of their relationship,' Officer Dixon went on.

I told them everything I knew and everything I thought I knew about Alice. I went into detail about the impression Jack gave me, and how I thought he was lying but had yet to prove it before he kicked me off the case.

'He hired me to find her to return a family heirloom,' I explained, 'but my gut tells me there's more to the story. I was about to withdraw from the case when he told me I was too late and he found someone else. Frankly, he gave me the creeps,' I added, for flavour.

I held my hands up as if to say, 'I don't know what else to tell you'.

Officer Dixon took a deep breath. 'Mr Cann has been charged with the attempted murder of Alice Kent.' And just like that, it was like a bomb was detonated in the interview room.

I sat stunned, mouth agape, for what felt like days but in reality was probably only about twenty seconds. I am not often speechless (ask my husband), but I was thoroughly struck by this news.

Like a montage from a movie, my conversations with Jack, the photos of Alice, all my thoughts and fears, every infuriating minute of agonising over this case zoomed through my mind as I sat there shaking my head.

'Can . . . can you tell me more?' I stuttered, knowing that it was rather unlikely.

I learned a few more details: their relationship was real, as I assumed it was, but about seven months ago, shortly after they moved in together, Jack had changed and become controlling and abusive. She put up with it for a while, but a few weeks previously she had escaped. She feared for her safety and, after receiving some very threatening messages from Jack, she contacted the police. Due to the content of the messages, they investigated Jack, and found the damning evidence.

I was told that Jack had contacted almost a dozen private investigators to track down Alice and the ring – which, as it turned out, did not exist. The police reverse image searched it and found the same picture in an auction listing from 2009. All but one of those investigators felt the same as me and declined the case. The one who did manage to find her passed on her location to Jack, who swiftly put the next part of his plan into motion. Fortunately, by this point, Alice had already contacted the police, and no attempt on her life was made.

For all the baffling parts of this case, I was the most shocked to have learned that, when Jack hired a hitman to kill Alice, he met him in a Costa Coffee. The banality of it fires a sickness in me to this day. Imagine discussing such atrocities over a flat white!

Rather unfairly (for me), the police wouldn't tell me how they found out about this, but irrefutable evidence would see Jack serve a sentence for this crime. There was no engagement, no family heirloom, no heartbroken ex. Just a very angry, abusive man who is now serving six years in His Majesty's Prison Service.

It turns out he never wanted a ring, he wanted revenge.

PI Perspective

I dread to think what would have happened if I hadn't trusted my intuition. I knew something didn't add up and I was almost certain that I couldn't trust what Jack was saying, which was quickly proven by a little due diligence.

I spent many hours scrutinising Alice's social media and researching as much as I could about her life. It would have been easy to make a lot of money from this case, but my integrity is much more important than a tidy payday – and nothing is more important than a person's life, which I am proud to say I played a small part in saving.

I like my cases to be wrapped up neatly and filed away. I like to be confident in the resolutions I find for my clients. But forming a solid conclusion on this case is tricky. After all, I didn't actually have any evidence, and *feelings* aren't admissible in court. Though ultimately, any evidence I could have found would have been unnecessary as the police had an entire investigation running alongside mine, but as someone who is desperate to find the truth, it still sits uncomfortably with me to this day.

My intuition has stopped me taking cases before and since this event, but I've never felt it quite so intensely as I did in this case – with Jack, in particular.

The cases we don't take are just as important as the ones we do.

CHAPTER 5

My Very First Case

Lesson #1 - All Dash-Cam Evidence Is Admissible in Court

I often think about the passage of time and am astounded by how it ebbs and flows. Somehow it feels like it was a lifetime ago that I first dipped my toes into this thrilling world, but also like no time has passed at all. I'm balanced between comfortable confidence in using my skills and techniques, and the unpredictability of experiencing something new with every case. There's been so much change, in both my personal and my professional life, that sometimes it's been a challenge to keep my head above water. But looking back on my very first case has shown me that I have learned a great deal over the last few years, both as a person and as an investigator. Reliving my rookie days gives me an unexpected sense of pride in just how far I've come.

It was all well and good deciding to become a private investigator; but actually doing it was more challenging than I had realised.

Growing up, it took me a while to find a learning style that really resonated with me. I absolutely hated school, and often struggled to keep up. Secondary school was particularly difficult – I don't know whether it was navigating becoming a teenager and the rebelling against authority that often comes with pubescence, or the fact that I just didn't care about what I was being taught (or the fact that my most of my teachers were uptight and dull, and their unengaging lessons would send me to sleep).

My mental health was on the decline during the latter part of secondary school, and as a result my grades were too. I scraped through and vowed to never have to look at a textbook again. Cut to a lifetime later, there I was, going back to school.

Well, not in the definitive sense; it was Open University, so I would be studying online. No stuffy classrooms, no horrible teachers, no bullies, and no excuses. If I didn't work hard, I might as well just throw my money away and save myself time.

I was still working full time, so I studied in the evenings. My daughter, Alexis, was in her early twenties, so I wasn't needed much in that area, and my husband, Mark, understood how important this was to me and afforded me as much time to study as he could. Even with the support, it was a huge, exhausting undertaking.

It helped that I found the subjects I was studying absolutely fascinating. From day one I was totally hooked on the course and the more I learned, the more I loved it.

As I completed each module, I found myself yearning for more information, so I dived into more subjects until I felt like I was ready to put the books down and get my hands dirty. Although in this particular job, I never stop learning; whether I'm wrapping my head around the vastness of the latest social media app (I'm looking at you, TikTok), or discovering new and increasingly grim aspects of human behaviour.

After I'd made it through all that, with my qualifications and certificates proudly displayed and my brain bursting with knowledge, it was time to go out and do it.

I decided to use my maiden name in business, partly to distance my work life from my home life, and partly to honour my dad, with whom I shared the surname Marsh. AM stands for Alison Marsh, Miss came as a nod to Miss Marple, and the investigations part is self-explanatory.

Thus, Miss AM Investigations was born. I'll forgive you for imagining me sitting with a half-smoked cigarette at a lonely, bare desk, with bars on the windows, a flickering ceiling fan, and wooden door with a frosted window with 'Miss AM Investigations' etched into the glass. To be honest, the reality was almost as bleak.

I'd spent so long learning to become a great private investigator, but I'd not spent a second learning how to start a business. It threw the excitement right out the window and I found myself feeling very lost.

One particularly glum afternoon, I was sitting in my freshly decorated office waiting for inspiration to kick in. My hands felt cold, reminding me that I needed to get a heater for this room, as I cupped my chin and rested my elbows on my desk.

I loved this space. Originally it was a large cupboard at the back of the house, but we extended the space and added some windows to make space for me to work. It was a cosy, modern office with raspberry red walls and a large window letting in natural light. Under the window was my desk, made out of dark wood – risky in a small space, but its confident colour against the bright walls emboldened me. It was sleek and imposing, yet minimalist; large enough to hold my laptop, some paperwork and a cup of tea. It was against the right-hand wall, so my black office chair with extra back support sat parallel to the door. Behind me was a bookshelf with my textbooks, novels, photos of me and the family, and a few plants, and next to it was a corkboard that I could flip over to be a whiteboard, depending on what I needed at the time. At my feet sat a brand-new dog bed for Barry, as I had suspected he might like it in there. My favourite part of my office was a sign on the door reading:

> ◦ **Never Underestimate a Pissed-off Woman** ◦

'You all right?' boomed Mark's voice, startling me. I turned my head to the right and saw him holding a teapot in one hand and a gin bottle in the other, holding them up as if to say, 'Which one?' I begrudgingly dipped my head towards the teapot. 'Good call,' I heard Mark say as he headed towards the kitchen, followed by the familiar and oh-so-comforting click of the kettle turning on.

I was relentlessly tapping my pen on my desk as I tried to plot my next move, with a creeping sense of panic making itself comfortable in the pit of my stomach. What if I didn't have what it takes? I had the knowledge and I felt like I had enough gumption to get the job done, but did I have enough steel in me to navigate the uncertain waters of running a business. I am my product, I am what I am selling – am I enough?

It felt like I'd eaten a doughnut made of lead, and this continued for a day or so, until I had a word with myself and snapped out of it. I hadn't come this far and worked this hard to falter now. I've invested a lot of time and money into this path and I'm damned well going to make it to the end, I vowed to myself.

Fast-forward a few weeks to spring of 2018, and I'd really found my stride. Miss AM Investigations was officially going, with a snazzy website, ads in all the right places, and my professional memberships all confirmed. I knew I needed resources from like-minded professionals, so I looked for somewhere I could find support and promptly joined the UK Private Investigators Network.

The UKPIN is a nationwide group of investigators sharing anything from one-of-a-kind cases to how to leverage Google ads for business, and everything in between. This was my best move and it opened up a world of knowledge to help me get moving.

It didn't take long for enquiries to start coming in. I promised myself I would vet every case before I agreed to it, and resist jumping at any chance to make quick money – a promise that I still keep to this day. Being ethical has always been at the heart of Miss AM and it always will be.

After a few dud enquiries, I received an email that looked promising. 'I've been scammed,' it began, which immediately piqued my interest. It went on to explain how she, Ginny, lent her friends a large sum of money for a house deposit. The friends had grand plans to do up the house and sell it on, making a nice profit, which they'd share with Ginny.

This was the sort of case I'd hoped to start off with; something that I could really flex my PI muscles with. After I'd read the email several times over, and made some notes of questions to ask, I responded to the email, suggesting a phone call or a face-to-face meeting to discuss further. Ginny replied almost immediately, giving me her address and suggesting some quiet places nearby where we could meet.

'I've done it!' I called out to whomever was listening.

Mark and Alexis both hurried to my office, their faces blank as they had absolutely no idea what I'd done.

MY VERY FIRST CASE

'I've got my first client meeting next week!'

We all cheered and I felt a huge weight lift off my shoulders – I could sense it from Mark and Alexis too. I felt like I could climb a mountain with all the adrenaline just from booking a meeting, I wondered how great it would feel to crack the case.

The following week came fast, and before I knew it I was heading out the door to meet Ginny.

I decided to drive there, although it was easily reachable by public transport, which I prefer to use when possible. I wasn't really sure what I was walking into, so the extra control driving gave me was important to me. I could feel my hands getting shaky as I gripped the steering wheel, but I tried to push past it.

'You will not mess this up. Just breathe. You've got this,' I said to myself. Followed by a bunch of expletives as I hit an unexpected amount of traffic. It was a twenty-minute drive on a good day, but, as luck would have it, today was not a good day. I hate being late and, even though I'd left in plenty of time, the traffic made me even more twitchy.

I was feeling hot and bothered, so I turned up the air con and the music in equal measure to help calm my nerves – singing along to the radio is the best part of driving somewhere alone, and I find belting out classics to the audience of my dashboard really soothing. The satnav beeped, indicating an alternative route, so I clicked 'accept' and was soon whizzing through the back streets until I reached my destination, with minutes to spare.

I pulled down the sun visor and inspected my reflection. I hadn't yet adopted my signature Miss AM look with bright red hair and bold glasses – I had shoulder-length brown hair with a slight fringe and a grey or two starting to show themselves. Several strands were refusing to behave themselves and my hasty attempt to smooth them into submission wasn't working. My cheeks were still glowing like stop lights from the stressful drive, so, after checking I still had enough time, I took a few moments to take some deep breaths and centre myself.

Once the fire alarms stopped ringing in my cheeks, I looked myself dead in the eyes and said, 'You're ready.'

We had chosen to meet at a small coffee shop, which would soon become my signature move. There's something rather comforting and anonymous about a coffee shop; the hubbub of conversations and warm scent of roasting coffee beans create a little bubble away from the outside world – the perfect setting for clandestine conversations.

I wasn't entirely sure of the etiquette here, so I ordered a pot of tea with two mugs and a selection of biscuits for us to share. I chose a table in the corner with firm-yet-comfortable red armchairs, close enough to have a conversation but not so close as to be imposing on each other's personal space. They were the only pieces of matching furniture in the whole place; everywhere else was mismatched shabby-chic style with tables and chairs of varying sizes and heights. Unsurprisingly for an establishment called the Vintage Roastery, its walls were lined in wallpaper adorned with different pink and white flowers and each table had assorted vases with peonies, carnations and roses that matched the walls. All of the wood was a dark, rich mahogany colour, scratched and faded (perhaps purposely) to fit in with the vintage style.

I tapped my fingers to the beat of the soft music playing in the background as I waited for my very first client to arrive. I didn't have to wait long before I was approached by an attractive woman dressed in jeans and a loosely fitted t-shirt with a floral pattern across the chest. She had a youthful glow but I could immediately see the stress in her face.

'Are you Ali?' she asked timidly.

I stood to greet her. 'Yes, I am. Ginny, I presume? It's lovely to meet you. I've got us some tea but if you'd like anything else please just ask.'

We sat down simultaneously. 'Tea is great, thank you,' she said softly as she picked up the pot to pour a cup.

She tucked a section of her short blond hair behind her ear but it immediately fell back across her face and she was visibly annoyed by it – a habit that carried on throughout our meeting.

We sat in silence for a few moments, neither of us quite sure where to start. This was an entirely new experience for both of us and you could sense our nerves from across the room.

'So . . .' we both said at the same time, making things even more awkward. She signalled for me to go ahead, so I asked her to give me the full story and tell me what she needed my help with.

'My friends' – she scoffed at the word – 'so-called friends are house flippers. They buy run-down properties cheap, do them up, sell them on for a profit. They've done about five houses so far and I've seen proof that it's a good money-maker.' Her tone was strained. It was as if she was defending herself before I even had the full story.

'About a year ago they found a property they wanted to buy, but the sale from one of their old properties hadn't gone through yet, so they were a few thousand pounds short and asked me if they could borrow it from me and they'd pay me back with the money from the other house plus interest – eight weeks max, they said.

'I know the house sale went through but when I asked them for my money back they went ballistic at me, calling me a terrible friend for asking when they were in such financial ruin. They said the business was going well but apparently they're absolutely skint. They made no money on the house they'd just sold and the one they're doing up is causing lots of problems.'

A small tear fell from her eye and she hurriedly swiped it away with the back of her hand, taking a big sniff. Again she tucked the same section of hair behind her ear and yet again it protested.

'Then they started harassing me, threatening me, and

just being awful. I think they're trying to scare me off so I don't ask for the money again, but it's MY money, it's not fair and I just don't know what to do. I talked to the police and they said I need proof but I don't know how to do that. Can you help me?'

Gathering evidence is a common undertaking for private investigators. We're trained to be fact-finders and have access to advanced tools and resources that members of the general population do not have. Beyond this, a PI like myself will have a breadth of legal knowledge to corroborate findings to ensure they are both reliable and admissible in court.

Often, legal proceedings are thrown out due to a lack of evidence, which makes this aspect of investigations critical and rewarding.

At this point, I hadn't learned to dig deeper before accepting a case, and I was so heartbroken for Ginny that I agreed on the spot.

'If I can, I will help you,' I said, placing a hand on her shoulder to comfort her.

She looked up at me with the saddest eyes and burst into tears. I'll be honest, I didn't expect such a raw emotional meeting as this, but although I was upset for her, it was validating to know that Ginny felt comfortable enough around me to let the wall come down.

'It's okay,' I told her – not entirely convinced it would be. 'Together I'm sure we can sort this out for you.'

We talked about what happened in greater detail,

and I learned that it was a loan of £8,000, taken out of an inheritance that Ginny had received when her grandmother passed away a few years previously. It added an extra layer of betrayal in her eyes, as her 'friends' knew that money came from such a loss, and that it was meant to set Ginny up with her own home, but instead it was stolen and she had no idea if she'd ever see it again.

When I was satisfied that I had enough information we parted ways, with a plan to meet up again at the same time next week.

As soon as Ginny left, the excitement and pride that was swelling in my chest could no longer be contained and I threw my hands in the air in celebration, shouting, 'Yesssss!' Not even the perplexed looks from the other patrons could faze me: I'd just booked my first investigation!

I drove home beaming from ear to ear, excited to get back and get to work.

I wanted to be methodical, so the first day on the investigation was spent planning every step. I sat at my desk listening to the gentle late-spring drizzle tapping on the glass. There was a light breeze, so every now and then a soft smattering of warm misty rain would sneak in through the slightly open window and gently dust across my workstation.

My plan was threefold: establish proof of the agreement between Ginny and her so-called friends; next, gather evidence of the harassment Ginny faced; and finally, prove that they did have the funds to pay her back.

I'd looked into similar cases and, so long as Ginny could show that they had originally agreed to pay the £8,000 back and that they could afford to – which hopefully my investigation would prove – then Ginny could settle this in the small claims court and hopefully get her money back. The harassment and intimidating behaviour could potentially bolster her case, so it was an important part of painting the full picture.

Prior to accepting my first case, I'd spent a few weeks consulting with other investigators and a solicitor to make sure my contracts were appropriate and accurate, with adequate protection for both myself and the client. In each contract I would outline my generic terms of service, fee structure and what was expected from both parties, and then I would tailor it for each individual case, outlining the agreed steps. I created this document for the first real case ready to send to Ginny, and upon her signed return the case would be live. It was such a thrilling – and utterly terrifying – time.

I'm fiercely independent, but at this moment, just before I hit send on the most important document of my career so far, I felt I needed a bit of emotional support. 'Mark?' I yelled from my desk. It was in the evening, two days after my first meeting with Ginny. I'd spent the first day creating my aforementioned plan, and the next I was at a seminar about forensic investigations, so this was the first chance I had to send them over to Ginny. I didn't want to be anything less than fully prepared, so I attached my full game plan to the contract.

He'd been cooking dinner, so it took a few minutes for him to come and join me and in that time I'd worked myself up so much I was practically bouncing off the walls with excitement.

'I'm about to send my first contract!' I beamed at him, and a wide, warm smile grew across his grey-stubbled chin. He put his cup of tea down (he is rarely seen without one) and rubbed his hands together in delight.

'Ok . . . aaaand sent!' We both cheered and then he went back to the kitchen while I sat there refreshing my inbox every ten seconds. Logically I knew it would take some time for Ginny to come back to me, but I couldn't help myself.

The excitement petered out as the evening drew on, and it was two full days before I heard back from Ginny. I know now that this is quite common; the contracts are quite long and can be a bit complex (depending on the case), but it is always a nail-biting wait.

She responded with great enthusiasm, which gave me a rush of relief and excitement for the next phase of the investigation.

Step one was digging deeper online. All I needed was some information from Ginny and a good internet connection to gather this first batch of evidence.

I'd asked Ginny to send me the details of her so-called friends, and screenshots of any emails and texts between the groups in which they discussed the agreement and finances. Next I needed the addresses of both properties and any proof of purchase they may have shared with Ginny. I also asked for a detailed timeline of the events to the best of her knowledge.

Ginny said she didn't know how to get the proof she needed, but she was very forthcoming with the information I would need to find it. From the first instance of them backing out of the deal, she started journaling every conversation and keeping record of every interaction.

Along with the information I'd requested, Ginny sent me screenshots of her damaged car and a video of her ex-friends (who I now knew were called Kirsty and Celia) shouting at her through her front door. Unfortunately it was difficult to see the person shouting, but it was a good starting point.

She also sent me proof of her transferring the money into Kirsty's account, which I'm a bit embarrassed to admit I hadn't thought of. I noticed that it was a personal account, not a business one, which I found rather strange seeing as they were supposedly professional house flippers.

I needed to know more about the houses themselves. If I could prove that the first house sold for a profit, or that renovations on the second house were going well, or even if I could prove the opposite, it would help paint a clearer picture of the situation as a whole. I scooted my chair closer to my desk to reach my laptop and opened it up. The screen burst into life, illuminating the room, which had turned dark as the clouds came over. It had been beautiful sunshine not even five minutes ago; classic unpredictable spring weather, I thought to myself as I reached up to the window to close it.

I opened up the browser and went to a popular real estate website. In the search bar I put the street address of the first house Ginny had told me about – the one they had just sold, allegedly for zero profit. This website is a font of knowledge for property prices, including recent bought and sold prices. I located the house in question and could see that it was sold for a whopping £90,000 more than it was purchased for. This didn't automatically mean that was profit, though; they could have spent more than that on the renovation, but every detail helps.

Next I needed to find evidence of the renovation itself. The website had photos of it after it was decked out, but there was nothing to indicate what it was like before. If they were professional flippers, surely this would be documented somewhere. Ginny wasn't aware of this, so I had to do some digging.

Instagram or Pinterest would be the best places to publicise a renovation as they are the most visual platforms, so I decided to start there. I searched 'home renovation hashtags' on Google to find the most popular tags to help whittle down my search.

At that moment, I felt like a real investigator. If I didn't hate having my photo taken, I'd have loved to have someone get a snap of this. My left hand was poised over my laptop, and my right hand holding my phone using just my thumb to scroll, eyes darting between the two screens, a pencil stuffed into my hairband. A flurry of pride and excitement washed over me as I dug deeper. This was what I'd been yearning for; what I'd worked so hard for.

It took quite some time to find what I was looking for. This early on I was barely proficient in social media – my courses taught me what to look for such as how to spot hidden details, or how to tell if an image has been digitally altered, and a subsequent social media basics course taught me how to look for it, but it was a slow start.

Eventually, after many wrong turns, I came across an account specialising in home renovations in the same area as the houses in question. After comparing some of the exterior photos, I discovered that this was the same property and the names on the account were Kirsty and Celia. Bingo!

Even in my novice days of social media, I knew that you should always be careful about how much you share online – especially if your profile is public, and even more so if you're lying about your finances.

I didn't have to look very far or spend ages trying to calculate the cost of each room in the house. It was much simpler than that; they said exactly what they'd spent on their Instagram. The total cost of their renovation, according to their recent post, was £58,000, meaning they had a rough profit of £32,000 – four times what they owed Ginny.

There was no real evidence to say that this was true, but as this information was made public, it would be admissible in court.

I conducted the same search for the newer property that they'd bought, and I could see how much they purchased it for, but there were no further details on the real estate site or on their Instagram.

A niggling voice in the back of my head told me to look harder, so I hopped onto the websites of a few local estate agents. I wasn't finding anything, but I had one site left to search. After putting in the street address and clicking 'search', I realised I had searched properties for rent, not for sale.

Well, luck was shining down upon me, as that accidental click took me to a property for rent, which just so happened to be the house Ginny had invested in.

The images on the listing were the same as on the sold listing on the other website, so it looked like they weren't renovating it, but rather that they were renting it out. Perhaps to gather some money to complete the project.

I dialled the agent's number and left a message for them to call me back, explaining that I was interested in renting the property and hopefully arranging a viewing. I could record the show-round and try to squeeze some information out of the agent, or perhaps the owners themselves.

I was practically fizzing with excitement! This was my

first time assuming a new identity to gather information for a case. I was glad I was being eased in gently with a telephone conversation before a face-to-face meeting, but this meant I had to have my persona locked in so there would be no inconsistencies.

For some reason, every single name in the English language left my brain at that moment, and I found myself tapping my pen on my desk trying to come up with one. Fortunately, I am now well versed in assuming a new identity at the drop of a hat, but that first time was difficult. I eventually landed on Kelly, a mum of two looking for a house to rent in a new area. Kelly is moving as her husband has started a new job and is finding the commute too difficult. Kelly's husband, Rick, works on the industrial estate a few miles from the house. It was the perfect ruse!

Sadly (for the case and for me/Kelly) this turned out to be a dead end as the agents didn't return my call. I left a few more messages and sent an email, but didn't hear back from any of them. I noted down Kelly's identity, in case I ever needed someone similar. The small binder in which I started a log of my cover stories that day is now bursting, and I make a point to look through it periodically to make sure I don't repeat.

'Right, that's enough scrolling for today,' I announced to myself while closing the lid of my laptop. I pushed back my chair and stood up – it was time to hit the streets.

*

One of the key takeaways from all my training was to always be prepared for anything. With this in mind, I grabbed my brand-new PI kit, which I had assembled a few weeks prior. In the bag was everything I would need to conduct surveillance. It was a lot smaller than it is now, as I've learned a few new tricks over the years.

The bag was an inconspicuous black handbag. It was lightweight but roomy, with plenty of pockets for keeping the various tools I would need in. I meticulously planned where I would put each item in order of how likely it was I would need it. My Dictaphone, a small video camera and my spare glasses were each in a pocket on their own. In a concealed pocket at the bottom of the bag I kept a change of clothes and a short blond wig in case I needed to quickly change my appearance. Then at the top, where it was most easy to access, I kept a make-up bag (partly to make it seem like a normal bag, and partly for other ways to change my appearance) and then two notebooks and ten pens. I'm forever stuffing pens in pockets or losing them, so it was essential to have plenty just in case.

The next logical step for this investigation was to go to the house myself and have a little snoop around. Of course I couldn't enter the house, but I could look around outside and see if there was much activity going on inside.

I was dressed casually, in muted colours, so I would blend in with anyone else milling about. I grabbed a light jacket in case the weather turned again, and my special

PI kit, and headed out the door, excited for my first real surveillance mission.

During my research of the house, I checked Google Street View to find the perfect vantage point to wait. I spotted a bus shelter across the road, which would be the perfect spot to look inconspicuous. I drove for approximately half an hour, entertaining myself with the radio as I so often do. I drove past the house and parked my car in a small car park adjacent to some shops about three roads away from my target.

As I got out of the car, I decided to peruse the little row of shops. Not only would I know the area a bit better, it would help me blend in a bit more. Someone parking up and walking away from the shops could seem suspicious, so I casually strolled along the parade and grabbed a hot drink from the cafe and a bottle of water and a magazine from the newsagents before walking the ten minutes to the bus stop.

You couldn't tell by looking at me, as I had a blank expression plastered on my face, but inside I was absolutely buzzing. This was completely thrilling – and I was at work! It still boggles my mind.

I'd checked the bus timetable before I left home so I could be sure to arrive shortly after a bus came, to give me plenty of time to 'wait' for the next one, making my ruse more plausible.

The house stood back about six feet from the street and had a small paved front garden. On a square of gravel in the middle were three matching terracotta plant pots – whatever was growing in them was in need of resuscitation. The front door was white uPVC – it looked relatively new and different from the picture online, so it was safe to assume they'd done at least some renovation on the house. Whether they went beyond replacing the front door remained to be seen.

The white facade of the house was in need of a coat of paint; years of being hit by all kinds of weather were apparent. It had watermarks from some leaking guttering and was flaking in some areas.

It looked like your typical fixer-upper and I understood why Kirsty and Celia were so keen to purchase it.

The sun shone brightly on the front of the house, making it difficult to see into the upstairs windows, but I could just about see into the downstairs, into what the floorplan on the estate agents' website told me was the living room.

Thanks to the open curtains and lack of blinds, I could see that the TV was on. I could just about make out a figure sitting on what appeared to be a sofa opposite the TV. According to the listing the house was unfurnished, so, from the time the listing was posted to now, someone had put in a sofa and a TV at the very least. I could have been mistaken, but it looked like someone was living there. Perhaps this was why my calls were not returned – the property was no longer vacant.

There were about twenty minutes until the next bus

was due, so I decided to keep monitoring the house until that point. The figure I could see in the window got up and walked to the back of the house, then back to the sofa. Up again to what appeared to be the upstairs bathroom, then back to the sofa. They moved around a few more times during my twenty-minute wait, but never to the front door where I could get a good look – it was just a faceless silhouette ping-ponging, around the house.

As the bus finally approached, I stood up and walked away back to my car, then home and to come up with my next steps.

Here's where I learned my first big lesson: if you're in a hurry to park because you're so excited to start your surveillance, survey the area for parking restrictions first. In my haste, I didn't notice it was a pay and display car park, and I returned to my car to find a bright yellow parking fine stuck to my windshield. I paid the £30 fine as soon as I got home and chalked it up to a learning opportunity – a mistake that I have thankfully never made again.

By the time I got home, dinner was ready and I was feeling quite wiped out from all the thinking and walking, so I took the rest of the night off. There wasn't much I could do now anyway and the last thing I wanted was to get burnt out already.

Over dinner, I eagerly filled Mark in on the case so far – innocently 'forgetting' to tell him about the parking ticket.

'Sounds like you're doing a great job,' Mark told me as I gathered the plates after dinner.

I felt elated. I hadn't realised how much I needed to hear that – I just hoped that Ginny felt the same. I couldn't wait to catch up with her the following day.

I called Ginny the next morning to update her on the investigation so far. I wasn't sure how often I should report back, but I decided to just go with my gut and only call when there were real developments.

Suspecting someone was living in the property and therefore Kirsty and Celia were making an income was definitely a real development.

I thought Ginny might be elated to find out that I was getting close to some real proof, but she just sounded absolutely devastated.

She let out a long, sad sigh down the phone when I told her the news and what I planned to do next.

'Part of me hoped this was a big misunderstanding and they really are struggling to pay me back,' she told me.

'I'm so sorry to have upset you, Ginny,' I said, feeling awful for sounding so elated at the development.

'No, no, please, it's not your fault. I just got my hopes up that they were still my friends, but I guess that's not true so it stings a bit.'

I told her I understood, I really did. It was already a horrible situation – she'd lost £8,000 and now she'd learned she'd lost some friends for good.

'But, I suppose this means there's a chance I could get my money back? If you can get more proof?'

'That's the plan!' I told her confidently.

When we finished the conversation, I kicked myself for having the entirely wrong demeanour. I didn't want her to suffer any longer, so I got cracking with the next, and hopefully final, phase of the plan.

My education had taught me that trailing people in my car would be a big part of the job. I'd studied it exhaustively and even practised a bit (only on Mark – I obviously didn't witness him cheating on me in the adultery sense, but I did catch him getting doughnuts twice and never bringing me any, which in my book is also very disrespectful). So I felt like I was completely prepared.

I was not prepared for how soul-crushingly boring it could be.

The aim of this surveillance was to establish that someone was definitely residing in the property for an extended period of time – not just temporarily. To do this, I would arrive outside the house early in the morning and wait for the resident to leave the house (most likely for work) and tail them there and back again. I'd do this over several days to establish a pattern of behaviour. I believed this would be enough evidence.

The sun and I rose at 5am. I went to bed early the night before but the anticipation of the following day kept me awake, tossing and turning until about forty-five minutes before my alarm. I was bleary-eyed and, quite honestly, in a bad mood. But needs must, so I shook it off, grabbed a strong coffee in a travel cup and headed out the door.

The sun was just peeking over the houses and hadn't quite reached my road, so my front garden and car were covered in a delicate dusting of dew. The spring air was so fresh that it gave me a chill as I stepped outside onto the patio and walked towards my car. As I sat in the car I let out a deep sigh and willed myself to get moving. I wouldn't have to start this early tomorrow, I reminded myself, but it had to be this way today so I could find out what time the tenant left the property.

I drove the short trip to the house and parked on the street opposite, a few car lengths away from the bus stop. Remembering my failure from last time I was here, I checked for any parking restrictions and could see none. It was a little before 6 by now, and I was already feeling the burn.

The hardest part of surveillance like this is focusing all of my attention on the subject, not letting myself be distracted by anything around me. Now, I've completed several hundred hours of surveillance like this, and I can say that it does get easier; I've found what works for me and I stick to that religiously. But in my novice days, I didn't really have a clue.

I waited. And I waited. And I waited.

It wasn't until around 7:30am that anything started to happen. I noticed a light peeking out round the curtains of the upstairs window. Quickly checking the printout I had of the floorplan, I saw that this was the main bedroom. Without taking my eyes away, I reached over for my camera, which was sitting on the passenger seat out of sight under a blue satin scarf. After a quick glance around to make sure no one was watching me watching the house, I snapped a few photos of the lit bedroom window – this would prove someone slept there overnight.

I felt like I had whiplash from the switch between the overwhelming boredom I felt just moments ago and this new feeling. I felt supercharged. The anticipation, the excitement and the satisfaction were overwhelming, and I had to calm myself down in order to carry on with my job.

'Enjoy this later,' I said to myself out loud. I had work to do; that had to be my focus.

At 8:04 the front door opened and I finally saw the full picture of the figure I had seen in the living room a week prior. He was a tall man with a muscular build, fair skin and slicked-back auburn hair. He was dressed casually, in beige chino-type trousers and a navy polo shirt. The shirt had an emblem on it, but from here I couldn't quite make it out. I'd hoped he'd be in a very obvious uniform to take some of the mystery out of the situation, as that would give me an idea of where we were heading, but no such luck.

For a moment, I had a stab of guilt – as far as I knew, this man was an innocent party in all this, and it felt slightly wrong to be investigating him. He wouldn't be implicated in any of this, I told myself, and my actions were purely to establish that someone was living there – not a blight on him personally. I didn't need to find anything about *him* per se, but I had to prove that *someone* was living there consistently. I pushed this feeling aside, and a sudden fear of being caught took its place. It was like being on a rollercoaster of emotions – unpredictable ups and down with a touch of nausea.

He got into a blue Ford Focus and sat in the vehicle for a few minutes before making any moves. I made a quick note of the licence plate just in case I lost him, as it was a very common car – three had gone past while I was sitting here.

He set off, and a few seconds later so did I. It suddenly occurred to me that he might be driving to the train station to get to work, and I panicked that I might have to come up with a contingency plan to get on the train if that was the case. I put that out of my mind for now, but made a mental note to remember that for future cases so I could be more prepared.

We pulled away from the house. I was immediately behind him, but kept back several car lengths. When we got onto a busier road, I let a few cars in front of me to maintain some distance. He had no reason to suspect he was being followed, but I think we're all guilty of noticing a car going the same way as us for a fair distance and wondering if they're following us for some reason – no, just me?

Fortunately, we drove straight past the station and a further ten minutes along the main road until he pulled into an industrial estate. There were five or six huge steel units with large shuttered entrances. The units were barely signposted, but I spotted signage that looked a little bit like the obscured logo on his shirt. I held back before turning into the estate's car park and then nipped in behind a lorry. As I had presumed he would, he parked his Focus outside the building with the logo on.

About forty minutes had passed, so I assumed he started work at nine. I parked up and grabbed my phone to look up the company's trading hours. They were open 9–5, which meant it was very likely that he would be here until 5pm, but I couldn't be certain. So, again, I waited. And waited. And waited.

By 1pm there was no change, and I had depleted all of my snacks and drinks, and was desperate for the toilet. I couldn't risk leaving and missing him, but it was getting dicey. So after a bit of quick thinking, I opened the app that corresponds with my dashcam and switched on the live feed option. I could now watch what my dashcam was seeing from my phone.

I hurriedly scuttled down the road to a small cafe on the other side of the estate, regularly checking the feed to make sure I hadn't missed anything. I made it there and back without missing anything, and I continued to wait. And wait. And wait.

The tiredness and boredom was really getting to me

by 5:30, so I was relieved when there was a mass exodus from the building, including our guy. The Focus left the car park and I followed after a further four vehicles. I knew where we were going this time, so I didn't need to stay so close. I opened all of my windows and cranked my music up to keep the tiredness at bay. I sang along to the best of country as we hurtled down the main road back to the house. Traffic was fortunately light, so we made it back in only thirty minutes. As I arrived on the street, the Focus had already parked, so I quickly stopped the car and snapped a few more pictures of him getting out and letting himself into the house with a key.

I was bone tired, so I drove straight home, uploaded the dash-cam footage to my laptop, and then flopped into bed. It's amazing how a day of nothing can be so exhausting.

I repeated the same for the following three days, but left home much later, as I knew by then that I didn't have to make sure I was super early to catch him.

At this point, I felt like I had captured everything Ginny would need. I gathered all of the evidence together, including the documents that Ginny had sent me such as bank statements, the message screenshots and the emails, as well as the social media posts, the estate agent listings, and the photos and dash-cam footage from the house. I prepared it all into a docket for Ginny and called her to arrange a time to meet.

MY VERY FIRST CASE

We met at the Vintage Roastery again, in the same red chairs, but this time Ginny beat me there and had ordered the same tea and biscuits as our first meeting.

'Here's everything,' I told her as I handed over a copy of all of the documents – I kept one too, filed away in my filing cabinet. It was quite an empowering moment for me, wrapping up my very first case. I felt a mix of emotions, but above all else I felt so proud. I shook my head in disbelief – had I actually done it?

I explained to Ginny what all the evidence signalled – that Kirsty and Celia had sold the previous house for a profit AND had a tenant in the new house. All of which should prove that they had a solid income and could pay her back.

Ginny was so appreciative and grateful for my hard work. It was a bittersweet moment, as from now it was entirely out of my hands and for me the case was finished. I was proud to have given her a good service, but a bit sad that it was all over.

We chatted for a while and she said she would let me know how everything went. I told her that I wished her all the best and that I really did care what happened.

'This is more than just a pay cheque for me, I hope you know that,' I told her as we said goodbye. She smiled and nodded, and we went our separate ways.

Weeks had passed and I had filled my time with a few little financial and fraud investigations – work was starting to come in steadily and I felt like I had really found my footing with it all.

I was enjoying a day off – it was sunny, so Alexis and I went down to the coast for the day. We were sharing a bag of chips on the sea wall, with our feet dangling in the sand and the sea air blowing us every which way, when my work phone rang – it was Ginny.

'Hello?' I answered, almost holding my breath in anticipation.

'Ali? I've got a court date! My solicitor said the evidence is brilliant and I've got a hearing to iron it all out!'

'Yes!' I shouted, knocking the chips out of Alexis' hands. She was fuming and we were about three seconds away from being swarmed by seagulls but I didn't care. I helped! I really helped!

After the hearing, Ginny and I planned to meet up near the courthouse to debrief. This time we met at the pub, because we would be either celebrating or commiserating. I wouldn't make it a habit to meet clients at the pub, but it seemed like an appropriate venue for this time.

I'd been waiting for about an hour before an elated Ginny burst through the door!

'Drinks are on me!' she cheered. 'Ali, we won!'

I shot up from my seat and we bounced in celebration. It was a triumphant moment for the both of us and I felt like I was walking on air.

She gave me a quick rundown of what happened in

court and explained that without my evidence she would not have won.

I felt a swell of pride in my chest, like it could burst at any minute.

'But Ali . . . did you know your dash-cam footage records sound too?' she asked, looking amused.

I blinked a few times, not quite understanding why she'd asked me this.

'It's just . . . Well, your rendition of "Jolene" by Dolly Parton was a particularly dominant part of the evidence-viewing in court . . .'

PI Perspective

I couldn't have asked for a better first case. The challenge that Ginny brought to me taught me so much about the investigator I want to be. I am so grateful to Ginny for trusting me to take care of such a difficult situation and allowing me to really stretch my wings and fly.

It's impossible to know whether Kirsty and Celia set out to rip Ginny off, or whether their circumstances really did change and they didn't think they could pay her back yet – although the evidence was to the contrary. Were they bad people or did they just make a bad choice?

Fortunately, after recovering her money, Ginny was able to move on but I have still not managed to get over the embarrassment of a courtroom full of strangers hearing me belt along to the best of country.

CHAPTER 6

Is No Proof Enough Proof?

Surely I'm Not Missing Something . . .

'I don't care what the evidence says. I'm telling you, she's cheating. Dig deeper.'

The call cuts off and I'm left staring at the screen. Investigations can be frustrating for all parties, but how do you move forward when all evidence suggests the client is wrong?

Jerry and Harriet had been married for thirty-five years – childhood sweethearts who lost touch but reconnected in their early twenties. Now creeping towards their late fifties, like many couples at that point they found themselves drifting apart. Harriet was home a lot less, citing working late or book club as two of the reasons; and this caused Jerry to become concerned about the state of their marriage. After over a year of agonising, he reached out to me for some answers.

He called me on a Thursday afternoon. It was during one of my very rare days off and I was in Oxford city centre for a spot of lunch and some retail therapy with my friends.

Hearing my work phone ring startled me as I wasn't working on a case at that time and typically people reach out to me via Facebook, email or the contact form on my website. They rarely call me in the first instance. I think this is because it's a little bit easier to send a vulnerable message if you're hidden behind a username. It's quite brave to actually pick up the phone and speak to a stranger about sensitive subjects.

I grabbed my phone out of my bag and examined the screen. It wasn't a number I recognised, which meant it could be a new client. I felt a small flutter of excitement and stood up to go and take the call.

'Ooh, Miss Marple's at it again!' laughed Diane, one of my dearest friends, who always lovingly makes fun of my job. I'm used to such quips, so I laughed along and then excused myself from the table and stepped outside.

It was a rare sunny day for south-central England, and the bars along the street were bustling. I nudged my way through the crowds, and made it to a quiet spot before the call rang off. I was greeted by a trembling male voice.

'Is that Miss AM?' the speaker asked.

'Yes, speaking, but feel free to call me Ali – can you tell me your name and how I can help you?'

'Hi Ali. My name is Jerry and I think my wife is cheating on me. Can you find out?'

IS NO PROOF ENOUGH PROOF?

It's a rather unpleasant topic, but catching cheaters takes up a significant portion of my workload. There are signs that, as an investigator, I've learned to spot a mile off. However, signs are not proof, and only hard evidence can confirm a suspicion. Mostly (though not always) when a client suspects their partner of cheating I have been able to prove them right one way or another.

I told Jerry that I sympathised with his situation and I would be glad to help, but I needed more information. Tucked down a small pathway in the middle of Oxford city centre was not the place for such a conversation, so I took his details, asked him to send me a brief email, and arranged to speak with him the following day.

Heading back to my table, the excitement of a new case wore off as the sound of Jerry's words repeated in my mind. He sounded so sad, and, while I am used to such cases, I will never get over hearing the dejection and vulnerability in people's voices. It's one of the trickiest parts of being privy to the harsh realities of someone's relationship.

'Right,' I announced, trying to get myself back into the day. 'Whose round is it?'

I got up the next morning with a dull ache in my head from one too many cocktails.

'That's what you get for going out on a school night!' my daughter, Alexis, said, laughing, as we crossed paths on the landing. A cup of tea, a glass of water and a packet of paracetamol was waiting for me in the kitchen, left out by my husband Mark before he left for work.

I fired up the grill, because the only cure for daiquiri-itis is a bacon sandwich.

After eating, I felt much more human, so I headed into my office.

The warm weather from yesterday had subsided, and been replaced with a dull, grey sky. The clouds were threatening rain, so I opened the blinds to let the little light from the day into the room. I find the rain so soothing, so I was looking forward to the downpour and watching it bounce off the wall of glass above my desk.

As I opened up my emails, my eyes looked for something from Jerry. There it was, as promised, but slightly less brief than I had anticipated. It began:

Nice chatting yesterday, as requested here is a little information about why I called you and why I need your help.

What followed was a long email, where Jerry poured his heart out to me. I spotted everything I would typically see in such cases; all the buzzwords were there. 'I fear we're growing apart', 'We've known each other since we were teenagers but I feel like we're strangers', 'I'm starting to believe there's someone else,' and, most gut-wrenchingly, 'I just don't think she loves me any more.'

In that moment I had deep respect for Jerry and the way

he'd opened up and made himself vulnerable to me. After all, to him I was a stranger. It's not uncommon for people to open up to me like this; one of the main characteristics of a good PI is making people feel comfortable talking about the things that are bothering them, almost like being an unofficial therapist. Usually people need slightly more encouragement to talk, but Jerry seemed desperate and was able to open up to me quickly.

As Jerry had given me a lot of details, I didn't need to dig much, so after spending about an hour rereading his email and making some notes of some of the key points he had shared with me I emailed him back as the first splodges of rain hit the window.

Hi Jerry.
Thank you for providing all this detail, it's very helpful. I'm sorry to see that this situation is hurting you and I will do my best to try to get you some resolution. I think the best way forward is for us to meet up to discuss. I see from your email that you're about an hour's drive away from me, so let's find a convenient spot in the middle for us to meet.

I made some suggestions and hit send, then read his original email again. His desperation was palpable, and from first impressions I would likely come to the same conclusion – that Harriet was cheating. But I would never say that for certain unless I had proof.

The timestamp on Jerry's first email showed that he'd sent it about forty-five minutes after yesterday's phone call, so I expected to hear back from him sharpish.

While I waited, I looked up Jerry and Harriet on social media. I like to have a bit of a look around before I agree to a case, but try not to delve too deep so I don't cloud my own judgement with any preconceived notions about my potential client or subject. It's much better to get everything straight from the horse's mouth, but a little due diligence such as verifying identity, confirming the relationship is real and so on helps.

Starting with Jerry's Facebook – which he conveniently included a link to in his email, and more conveniently was a public profile so I could see everything – I could immediately tell he was still besotted with his wife. His profile picture was the two of them on a beach, on holiday, I presumed. All but one of his photo albums had something to do with Harriet, mainly various trips and even an album of their wedding photos, which appeared to be a mixture of scans and photos of printed photographs. It made me smile thinking about how he painstakingly scanned/photographed all fourteen of those images. The only album without Harriet was entitled 'Golf Trip' and included almost fifty photos of various men (Jerry included) posing at various golf holes, in golf carts and the like.

Jerry seemed like your typical fiftysomething British bloke. He liked golfing, having a beer with friends, sharing not-very-funny memes, going on sunny holidays and his wife. A 'classic boomer', my darling Alexis told me when she popped her head into my office while I was browsing his profile.

Harriet, on the other hand, kept her cards very close to her chest. Her account was easy to find as she was tagged as Jerry's spouse on his profile, but she didn't really post much. Most of the photos on her account were tagged photos from Jerry's, and she didn't display her marital status.

That's not typically a red flag without more detail. Often people choose not to display their marital status, or sometimes they just don't fill it in when creating their account. There could be many reasons, but I file that thought into the back of my mind to come back to later if necessary.

My search was interrupted by my phone's alarm. I typically only allow myself an hour of digging before taking a case, and set myself a timer so I don't dig too deep. That hour has flown by and I was surprised to see I hadn't heard back from Jerry yet. Not uncommon, but he'd seemed so keen, I had expected to know how we'd be moving forward by now. I decided I'd take advantage of this rare quiet period and closed my laptop.

There was a break in the rain, so I grabbed my dear old dog Barry and took a stroll up the road.

About ten minutes' walk from my cottage is a small parade of shops. To get there, much to Barry's excitement, we cut through a small field. Just as we turned down the pathway, where typically my phone loses signal, I quickly refreshed my email inbox. 'Nothing – ' I began to say out loud, but then Barry's patience ran out and he tugged me towards the field, knocking the wind right out of me.

After a few laps round the field, I meandered round the shops for half an hour. Before heading home, I popped into the bakery and grabbed fresh cream cakes for Alexis and me, and an egg custard tart for Mark. Barry looked thoroughly betrayed, so I grabbed him a pup-cake too, then headed home, avoiding the field – my lungs couldn't take another turn and nor could Barry's legs.

We got home just as the rain began again. It was hammering down now, and I could hear it on the conservatory roof like an out-of-time drum as I clicked the kettle on. Another quick email check – still nothing.

This went on for days – both the rain and the waiting. I don't know which was more irritating. Both were frustrating, but I could only do something about the latter.

I'm never shy about picking up the phone, but I try not to chase clients, especially with delicate matters, as I don't want to come across as too pushy. But four days with no response was bizarre, more so because Jerry seemed so keen from the off. Either he didn't get my email, or he did and he'd changed his mind. I'd never coerce, but equally, if he hadn't got it, I'd have hated for him to think that *I* was ignoring *him*.

IS NO PROOF ENOUGH PROOF?

I sat in my office, leaning back in my chair, then forward, then back again, trying to get comfortable. I dialled Jerry's number and lingered over the call button.

DING.

In comes an email from Jerry.

Ali, I can only apologise, your email ended up in my junk folder, would you believe?!

I couldn't help but laugh to myself. Technology, eh?

He selected one of the options I had given and we arranged to meet the following day.

'I was doing everything I could to keep the spark alive,' Jerry told me when we met face to face. He had a comforting nature and seemed very warm and open, just as he had seemed over the phone and email. Thinking back to his Facebook profile, I noticed he had the same smile and sense of style as his photo, but his hair was a little more salt-and-pepper, and the lines round his mouth and eyes looked deeper.

He told me in his email that he didn't want to go anywhere too enclosed, so we met at a park that I had suggested, about a twenty-minute drive from his house. He seemed very anxious, as if he had done something wrong, nervously picking at the lid of his takeaway coffee cup. It was making an aggravating clicking noise, but I ignored it and focused on what he had to say.

'I thought we were making progress; she certainly seemed a lot happier than she had for well over a year.'

He explained how as Harriet approached fifty – about three years before he reached out to me – she started to pull away. The first thing he noticed was that their sex life had all but disappeared.

'I know we're getting to "that age" and we've known each other for decades, but there was still a lot of romance and spark. We . . . you know . . . we were together fairly regularly . . .' He signalled air-quotes when he said 'together' and looked rather awkward to be bringing it up. I, of course, knew what he meant, so I nodded sagely and didn't press him further.

'Then all of a sudden, that stopped.' He took a long pause, chewing his lip as if trying to piece it all together in his mind. 'Actually no, it wasn't sudden, it's been a slow, drawn-out process and now here I am, convinced she's having an affair – or affairs – and I just don't know what to do any more.' The catalyst for reaching out, he told me, was when Harriet missed an important family event, which was completely out of character for her. He slumped his shoulders and wrapped his arms round himself as he slowly shook his head. He grasped tight as if his brown trench coat was his armour, not only protecting him from the light rainfall but from the pain he was feeling. I placed a sympathetic hand on his shoulder to encourage him to go on. He took a deep, determined breath, looked me in the eyes and continued telling me his story.

IS NO PROOF ENOUGH PROOF?

I walked away from our meeting, fighting the urge to give him a big, reassuring hug as I left. I've spoken with countless men and women who are convinced their spouse or partner is cheating, but I've never met someone quite as beat-up as Jerry.

As I've said before, I like to go away and think about a case before I accept. But Jerry's case seemed quite straightforward, so I told him there and then that I would gladly try to help him. We talked about the process, the fees, the agreement between us, and what my next steps would be. I promised to send over the contract when I got back to Oxford in a few hours.

I was pretty wiped out from the journey and the long, emotional conversation, so, after I'd spent some time hunched over my laptop getting the necessary documents ready for Jerry, I had a quiet dinner and then took myself off to bed early, so I'd be ready to tackle the case in the morning. Just as I grabbed my phone to silence notifi-cations, an email came in from Jerry with a long thank-you message and signed contracts attached. Next my banking app alerted me to money hitting my account – Jerry's deposit – then I switched my phone off and was practically comatose as soon as my head hit the pillow.

I expected to wrap this case up within a week, as I often do with cases of this nature, but I had no idea just how challenging this investigation would be.

Being cheated on by a partner is one of the most hurtful and humiliating experiences imaginable. Suspecting that your partner is being unfaithful can cause a lot of distress, and if it turns out to be true it can turn your entire world upside down.

While, thankfully, I can't speak from personal experience, I've learned over the past few years by speaking with my clients who have been cheated on (and those who have cheated) that the act has a ripple effect; the impact can be felt by all those involved and even those who aren't.

Over half of the enquiries I receive are from people concerned for the future of their relationship, fearing their partner is being unfaithful. I wish I could say it's a waste of everyone's time, but unfortunately often the culprit is caught red-handed. Often – not always. There are some instances where there is simply no substantial reason to definitively say there is anything untoward going on. While the news of a cheating partner is heart-breaking, I believe it's best to know for sure, and every former client of mine whose cheating partner I have exposed would agree.

Proving infidelity is not as simple as snapping some photos of them in a restaurant and calling it a day – cheaters are clever, manipulative and sneaky. It's more than catching them in the act; a snap of them being close, kissing, holding hands and so on is simply not enough. Things like that can be explained away – after all, cheaters are often champion gaslighters – so there's a systematic approach to finding real proof of the lies, the deceit and the other miserable facets of adultery.

For this particular case, I first had to establish whether Jerry's suspicions held up. Could there be a simple explanation for Harriet's behaviour? I find it easier to seek alternative explanations rather than jump straight to infidelity. Having a more openminded view of the situation adds a clarity that would otherwise be clouded if I went straight to accusations. For all I knew, Jerry could just be reading too much into the situation, although I had never seen someone so convinced as he was.

The plan was to track Harriet's movements to corroborate her excuses for being out all of the time, and to see if any of the patterns Jerry had told me about were coincidence or something to investigate. The first step would be to monitor her comings and goings for a week, so I made a call to a well-trusted associate of mine who handles such aspects for me, and arranged to have a GPS tracker fitted to Harriet's car.

In the UK, there is no specific law regarding GPS trackers; however, there are several key regulations that govern its use as a surveilling tool. The main regulation related to this is the Data Protection Act. For a tracker to remain ethical, and not breach any acts, rules or regulations, it needs to be completely anonymous. Who the device is tracking is on a strict need-to-know basis (in this instance, myself and Jerry) and any data it collects must be secure, encrypted and deleted after thirty days. No identifying information whatsoever can be stored – for example, I couldn't use details like Harriet's name, physical attributes or address on the records. All my trusty associate knew was the make and model of the car, and where it would be located – to do this I use the What Three Words method to give a precise location without giving street names or postcodes.

There are a lot of hoops to jump through to remain legal and ethical – this is something I pride myself on and, if I ever feel a case may cross a line, I'll drop it immediately.

You may wonder why I don't simply attach the tracker to the vehicle myself to cut out the middleman and add an extra layer of data security. This certainly would help to ensure anonymity; however, the simple and honest answer is that I just do not want to. The installer needs to lie under the car to get the device into the right spot and this does not appeal to me one bit! Moreover, I'm fairly certain I wouldn't be able to get back up again. I just know I'd have to lie there for however long until they drove off, and pray someone came along to heave me off the tarmac. Wily I may be, but agile? Not so much.

The tracker was booked to be installed in the next few days, so I let Jerry know what would be happening and he arranged to inconspicuously borrow Harriet's car for a day so my guy could do his thing.

It's remarkably easy to monitor a person's whereabouts with a GPS tracker. My associate will attach a small, discreet device to Harriet's vehicle (or it can go in a backpack or similar) and then connect to it using a laptop or phone. You have to be nearby for the initial connection, but from then on the vehicle (or whatever item you've attached it to) can be monitored from anywhere. GPS trackers use satellites to determine a user's location in real time – similar to a satnav but in reverse.

Once the connection was established, I was able to access the tracker's data and watch Harriet's movements. Jerry had provided me with three locations that Harriet had told him about, and asked if I could corroborate her stories by proving (or disproving) that was where she was. He also gave me a handful of addresses that were not red flags, such as her work, her sister's house and her best friend's house. He said any addresses other than those were cause for concern. I felt this was a bit broad, as people often nip off to places, try new coffee shops and so on, but I went ahead as requested.

Have you ever seen the game *Pong*? It was one of the first computer games ever created, and in it a white circle (denoting a ping-pong ball) would float from one side of the screen to bounce off the other. Revolutionary at the time! Well, tracking Harriet's movements was very much like that.

Home – PONG – work – PONG – home – PONG – local coffee shop – PONG – home – PONG and so on. I can honestly say it was the most boring trace I've ever seen.

Whether it was book club at the local arts centre, Pilates class at the gym or a visit to see her sister and nieces, every event she told Jerry about was substantiated.

It was Thursday at around 1.45pm – four days into the trace – and Jerry called me in a panic.

'It's time!' he announced. 'She said her gym class was cancelled so she's joining another one – but I bet she's off with him!' It was a bold claim, and I told him so, but I agreed to check to see Harriet's location. Unsurprisingly to me, she was at the gym. I checked the timetable and I could see the 5pm class had indeed been cancelled, so, it appeared, she was at the advertised 2pm session instead.

We had a long conversation and I explained that so far the trace didn't support any of his suspicions, and that what Harriet had been telling him was right.

'Well, it hasn't been the weekend yet! Just wait, you'll catch her!'

His behaviour was starting to alarm me slightly; I knew he was desperate, but this was bordering on obsessive.

The weekend came and went, and still no signs of Harriet not being where she said she would be. Uncharacteristically, she didn't go out with her friends on Friday night as Jerry had expected, and he sounded completely devastated when he told me that – I suspected he thought that was his last shot at catching her.

He was still begging for answers and I didn't know where to go next. I just had to keep searching.

IS NO PROOF ENOUGH PROOF?

The wind was blowing from the west, carrying the joyful sounds of kids playing in the local school. It must be morning break, I thought to myself. Which means I've been sitting here staring at my screen for two hours, making absolutely no progress.

I notice that I'm picking at my nails; a little habit that only comes out when I'm feeling particularly flustered. I need to find a new lead, or a new avenue to look down, because everywhere I've looked so far has been a dead end.

None of the evidence was pointing towards Harriet cheating. Jerry said his main concerns were that she was going out a lot, she had joined a gym, and she went to a book club once a week, and out with friends every weekend. So far, I'd discovered all of those excuses to be legitimate.

Am I really missing something, or is he wrong? I know what I *think* but I have to prove it. At this point I was quite convinced that Harriet was not cheating, a far cry from my original hypothesis, but Jerry was just not having it. It just goes to show that no matter what I assume at the beginning, nothing is concrete without evidence, and it can be easy for my opinion to shift as the case progresses.

He asked me to do another week of tracking her car, but I told him honestly that it would be a waste of his money, and that instead I would steer the investigation another way.

It was time to join the book club.

Thankfully it was a public book club at an arts centre

near where Jerry and Harriet lived, so it didn't take much to get a spot – just one phone call. I made the call on Monday and was invited along to the session that Wednesday. This wouldn't give me enough time to get everything prepared, so I pushed it back to the following week and secured my spot.

'We only have one rule – as I guess many clubs do!' Elaine, the bubbly administrator of the club, told me: 'You must have read the entire book within the week! Or listened to the audiobook if that's your preference, but we don't like to spoil things for people, so we insist you must have completed the story.' It seemed like quite an intense group, as they read a new book every week. I presume that was why it was easy to get a spot – not many people have the time to commit to a whole book in a week.

I love reading and I can knock a book out in just a couple of days (I wish I could say the same for writing one!). The book this time was *The Seven Husbands of Evelyn Hugo* by Taylor Jenkins Reid, which was conveniently already on my to-be-read pile. I scanned my cascading bookshelves looking for it, recalling it had a black spine with white writing. I slipped it from good company between other Taylor Jenkins Reid titles that I had already finished, and got to it.

The book has many themes, but primarily it's about how relationships can come and go in ways you might not expect. It's about love and connection, as well as mistrust and obligation.

IS NO PROOF ENOUGH PROOF?

They're doing the hard work for me, I thought to myself, as the book touched on topics that would be easy to crowbar personal stories into to encourage Harriet to open up – that was the plan, at least.

I had nine days until the book club and I finished reading it in five, leaving some time to dig deeper into who Harriet was (or portrayed herself to be) via her social media.

Often, women of a certain age have a very typical Facebook persona, and it's usually quite accurate to who they are in real life, so, while I took everything with a pinch of salt as I always do with social media investigations, I could trust that most of what she shared was realistic.

And that was, well, barely anything. I'd already had a glance at her profile before I agreed to take the case, and it was slim pickings there, but this was a deeper dive and I hoped to understand her a lot better. This turned out to not be the case, as she shared things I already knew. Every Wednesday she 'checked in' at her book club, and included a short review of the book they'd been discussing. A few times a week she shared that she was at a local cafe, which I learned was also a bookshop. I knew from Jerry's summary that she 'went for coffee' a few times a week, and to him that was concerning, but my research led me to believe she went to this particular place as it was a hot spot for avid readers, and she would go there to dive into her book ready for the following Wednesday's session.

I scrolled through countless shared posts of competitions (she *really* wanted to win a Fortnum & Mason hamper) as well as cutesy gifs from various holidays throughout the year – Easter, St George's Day and so on. The only thing she consistently talked about was book club; it clearly meant a lot to her. I felt a jab of guilt that I would be sneaking in, and hoped that she wouldn't find out. I wasn't going with any malice, I was just investigating, but I wouldn't have wanted to ruin this for her.

I'd gone back about eight months when I spotted a Facebook advert for a group for her local gym's Pilates sessions: 'Fab & Fifty Fitness'. While I loathe social media in my personal life, and hate how invasive it can be when pushing targeted ads, I thanked it at this point for giving me a lead.

On clicking into the group I could see that at the beginning of the year there was a fitness challenge, and Harriet had joined it. Her comment on the post read, 'I'm a bit over 50, so I hope I still qualify. To be honest, I've lost myself, and I don't know what to do about it. I've read that Pilates is good for the body AND the soul, so maybe this is what I need.'

To the untrained eye, this might seem like nothing, but to an expert in human behaviour and psychology this is an answer to a complicated question.

It was becoming increasingly clear that Harriet was not having an affair, she was having an identity crisis and was doing the work to feel better. At that moment, I applauded her. In the midst of a personal crisis, it's hard to realise that something isn't right, and even harder to do something about it. I was so proud of this woman who I had never met but seemed to understand so well.

That's an all-too-common thought for an investigator – you learn so many things about someone you'll probably never meet, and it's a strange feeling to make such a one-sided connection.

I felt that the investigation could easily wrap up here, but I was not convinced that Jerry would agree. While I had a very good idea about the situation, I had no proof, so I still attended the book club as planned.

I travelled down to the small London suburb in which Harriet and Jerry lived. Right in the centre was the arts centre that held the book club. Just outside was a small coffee cart, so I grabbed myself a hot chocolate before heading inside, always keeping an eye out for Harriet. She, of course, had no idea who I was, but I still dressed slightly disguised.

I think, regardless of the case, it's important to keep some form of anonymity. Whether it be dressing differently, prosthetics or wigs, I have an arsenal of ways to change up my appearance when needed.

I didn't go too drastic, as sometimes that can draw more attention. I kept my red hair on show, but put a large headband in and pinned up some of the longer bits to make it look like a different style. Swapped out my large glasses for smaller rimless ones, swapped my hoop earrings for small studs, and contoured my jawline to make it look more square. Small changes but they made a big difference – not only did I look different, it helped me really embrace the persona I was using that evening.

I was playing the role of Claudia, a book-loving legal secretary, who – after recently divorcing – was looking to find herself after such a life-altering event. Claudia's ex-husband, John, grew increasingly suspicious of her and she realised she had fallen out of love with him and so decided to leave.

With hot chocolate in one hand, and the book under the other arm, I headed into the book club.

As soon as I opened the glass double doors to room 5 of the arts centre, I was hit by a wall of noise. About twelve people of varying ages and genders were gathered in small groups having a friendly natter. It seemed like everyone knew everyone and I felt a little lost – like an outsider – but I pushed Ali's feelings aside and carried on as confident Claudia. I was waved down by a small, stocky woman with tight whitish-blond curls, dressed smartly in loose-fitting chequered trousers and a pink blouse.

'Ah you must be Claudia!' she announced, to myself and to the room. She didn't give her name but I knew from the voice that she was Elaine, the kind club administrator I had spoken with last week.

She looped her arm in mine (a little close for my liking but I couldn't be seen to be stand-offish so I went with it) and walked me over to the first small group. Each person introduced themselves to me and said they were pleased to have a newcomer in the group. Just for one week, I thought to myself, with a small jab of guilt.

I'll be honest, as I write this I realise I can't recall a single name, but everyone seemed so friendly I made the effort to remember them for the evening. As we got to the second group, I felt all the hairs on the back of my neck stand up. Harriet was right in front of me. I gave her a quick but subtle scan and noticed that she appeared a little older but more svelte than she did in the pictures I had seen of her previously. No doubt thanks to weekly Pilates.

Aside from Elaine, she was the most friendly person in the room. She came across so warm and welcoming, not the cold, negative woman Jerry had described her as having become.

She had dark brown shoulder-length hair with grown-out copper highlights. It flicked out at the ends in a chic way that looked effortless but probably took a few swipes of hair straighteners to achieve. She was dressed casually, in beige linen trousers and a thin light-blue jumper. A long corded necklace with a beautiful blue glass emblem hung from her neck and complemented the blue of her jumper.

'We haven't had a newcomer for a while,' she said, beaming. 'Claudia, is it?'

'Yes, I'm Claudia, and I'm thrilled to be here,' I said, trying to mimic her buoyant tone.

The hubbub settled and everyone began to take their seats. Elaine beckoned me over with a little tap on the chair next to her, but I wanted to be as close to Harriet as possible so I pretended I didn't clock her and took a seat on the opposite side of the circle. Elaine looked a bit put out but appeared to brush it off, and began the session.

To start, everyone took it in turns to give their initial review of the story, but other than that there wasn't much structure to the session, which made it easier to shoehorn in thoughts to support my investigation. I pulled out my notebook, which held my late-night scrawls from my long reading sessions.

Discussions began around Evelyn Hugo's 'morally grey' persona and how her actions are a reflection of how humans can be imperfect. Then we got on to how the character shows you can learn from your mistakes and grow or change, no matter how old you are.

It was my turn to chime in.

'I actually can relate to Evelyn quite a lot,' I began, grabbing everyone's – notably Harriet's – attention. 'Through good and bad relationships, I've learned that ultimately *I* am the person I should be looking after the most and my needs are important. It's like she said: "They are just husbands, I am Evelyn Hugo", which really helped me come to terms with my recent divorce. I lost myself, but I've found her again – does that make sense?'

I scanned the room, leaving my gaze on Harriet, who

was chewing the inside of her lip as if to stop herself from screaming, 'ME TOO!'

The focus turned away from me as the group discussed my comments and how looking at it that way changed how they felt about Evelyn. I sat back and took it all in until I heard a little voice next to me.

'Claudia, how did you do it?' Harriet asked.

'Do what?' I said, pretending I hadn't teed up this exact conversation.

'How did you discover you had to leave to find yourself again?' she asked shyly. I hadn't said that, I'd said I was divorced but never gave specifics; it seemed she was hearing what she wanted so she could ask what she needed to know.

At that point, we were interrupted by Elaine calling for our final book rating – I gave it eight out of ten. She then said that, as a newcomer, I could choose next week's book. This was so awkward as I didn't plan on coming back, but, in case I had to, I chose something I knew cover-to-cover – *Murder on the Orient Express* by Agatha Christie. I smiled to myself at the irony of choosing an investigator – no one would know why and that gave me a little thrill.

'Ok, that wraps up this session but there's drinks coming out shortly – Claudia, I hope you can join us!'

I stayed, of course, to finish my conversation with Harriet and wrap this case up.

'I daren't say it out loud. I haven't told anyone about this but you seem to feel the same and I'm hoping you can help,' she told me mysteriously over a glass of (cheap) white wine. She leaned against some metal racking filled with books – titles the book club had covered, I assumed.

'I – gosh it sounds so silly,' she traded further. I sipped my wine patiently and encouraged her to go on.

'I don't think I like my life very much. I've been really unhappy for some time now and I've tried different things to feel better – more me – but nothing helps. I've joined a bloody gym, for goodness' sake!'

I, Claudia, sympathised with her and said I had felt the same before, too.

'I think the problem is Jer, my husband. I think I've outgrown him.'

Ooof. That felt like a gut punch to me, so I dreaded to think how Jerry would feel.

'Have you tried talking to him about it?' I asked, knowing the answer already.

'I just don't think he cares. He hasn't said a word about the gym or this book club, or that I make any excuse possible to be out of the house. He would probably think I was having an affair if he ever put down his bloody phone to notice I'm never there.'

This, right here, is why not everyone can do what a PI does. I kept a completely straight face at the affair comment, while in my head absolutely cracking up.

'Well, are you?' I asked speculatively.

'Absolutely not, I wouldn't dream of it. But I do dream

about leaving.' She hung her head as if she was ashamed.

My heart broke for Jerry and for Harriet. This whole case could be chalked up to misery and misunderstanding. I encouraged her to talk to Jerry about it herself, and she said she would in the coming weeks. I wasn't sure if she would, but Jerry would know either way before she got the chance, as I planned to deliver the results of my investigation the following day.

We spoke for a while longer about how she was feeling and I committed as much as I could to memory, until the event came to a close and we said our goodbyes.

'Thank you, Claudia. I know you came to talk about books and I ended up blurting my whole life at you. I look forward to seeing you next week, and thanks again.'

I told her that I appreciated her confiding in me and that I hoped to see her again. I knew I wouldn't, but she didn't need to know that just yet.

Next I had to talk to Jerry.

I knew I wouldn't be up to driving home that evening, and had booked a room in the hotel opposite the arts centre. When I got to my room I was exhausted, but I still had work to do. I sent an email to Jerry asking him to meet up with me tomorrow. He quickly replied with

Yes – same as last place? I can do 10am.

Once that was confirmed, I typed up everything I could remember from my discussion with Harriet and put it together with what Jerry had told me about his feelings on the situation. Jerry was stubborn and very committed to the idea of Harriet being a cheater, so I had to be crystal clear with my assessment. Once I was sure, I nipped to the hotel's business centre to print it all out so I could physically give Jerry the answers – having a tactile handover can really drive the message home, and I hoped this approach would work with Jerry.

He was already waiting for me as I approached the bench the following morning at 10am. It had only been a few weeks since we last sat there, but the temperature had dropped and seasonal changes were becoming noticeable in the trees.

Jerry looked concerned, and I took a deep breath to steel myself before the difficult conversation. He stood up as he saw me approach, and I waved for him to take a seat and get comfortable.

I didn't want to bury the lede and keep him hanging, so I jumped straight to the conclusion, planning to then explain how I got there, point by point.

'I can confidently say that Harriet is not having an affair,' I told him.

I expected him to interrupt me to argue, but he just looked at me with an expression that was difficult to interpret, so I carried on.

'I know you were sure that she was, and I can understand why. Her behaviour changed and she became distant, especially with the increased socialising and gym visits. Typically these are red flags, but, after thoroughly investigating, I've discovered that . . .' I paused. This was going to be hard.

'This isn't going to be easy for you to hear,' I said, placing my hand on his shoulder in comfort.

Then I told him everything.

I was braced for a big reaction, but he just looked at the floor and said, 'Ok, thank you for your time.'

I gave him the docket of information I had gathered, and he took it slowly, still not making eye contact with me. A whole range of emotions must be running through him at once. Heartbreak, loss, sadness, shame – all fighting for top spot.

He still couldn't look at me when we parted ways. He thanked me again, and I found myself apologising for not having better news. But what would have been better? I mused upon this the whole way home. Would it have been easier if Harriet had met someone else? I guess that way Jerry would have been absolved of any blame. As far as I could tell, he hadn't done anything wrong, but sometimes when relationships span decades and countless life events, people change and, in this case, they fall out of love.

When I got home, I made sure to give Mark an extra-long hug. He was suspicious, but gladly accepted my embrace.

And that's case closed on Jerry and Harriet.

PI Perspective

In my professional experience, every person who has come to me with suspicions that their partner is cheating has been proven correct. A YouGov survey conducted several years ago showed that 20% of participants admitted to cheating on their partners and I would suspect that number will rise – if it hasn't already.

Whenever I pick up a new cheating case, I often think about Jerry. His case was rather unique in that it's the only time I have proven that someone isn't cheating. I think about whether I handled the conclusion correctly – should I have just said that I was sure Harriet wasn't cheating and left it at that? Did I *need* to tell him what she said? I always come to the same conclusion – Jerry asked for my help, and giving him ALL of the answers, no matter how painful, was the ethical thing to do.

Telling someone that their wife isn't cheating, and exposing the reasons for her behaviour changes, was equally as distressing as telling someone their wife IS cheating. People get hurt, and that's just something any good PI has to get used to. The bad news is just as important as the good news.

CHAPTER 7

Hidden Assets

Attention Gaslighters: I Will Outsmart You

Trying to prove infidelity is high-stakes at the best of times. I always strive to find closure for my clients and do what I can to help them heal and move on. But when the life someone has spent building for decades comes into question, getting a win is more important than ever.

'I know he is cheating on me, I just need evidence so I can divorce him,' Suzanne, my potential new client, told me over video chat. While I much prefer a face-to-face meeting, on this occasion it wasn't possible, so we settled for digital.

She'd reached out to me three times by now and every time she cancelled before we could meet. Cold feet is very common, especially in investigations like Suzanne's where legalities and abuse are a key part of the case.

I thought about not responding when I received her latest message. It had only been a month since our last failed attempt at meeting and I wasn't in the best place (emotionally) to deal with the high of meeting a new client and the low of them not turning up, especially as there was a great distance between us. I knew deep down that I would never forgive myself if something happened to her that I could have prevented. It was frustrating but I felt that I needed to see this through.

'This time is different, I just can't take it any more.' She assured me that she did want to go through with the investigation, and I believed her.

Over several phone calls and messages spanning the last few months, I had pieced together quite a bit of information regarding the situation she was in.

I learned that Suzanne and Paul lived in Scotland with their daughter, Charlotte. Suzanne was born there but moved to England for work in her twenties. When she and Paul got married they decided they wanted to raise their family back in Scotland to be closer to Suzanne's relatives.

When they entered into the marriage, Paul had a significant property portfolio and Suzanne had only a small one-bedroom flat to her name. They agreed, for the sake of fairness, to sign a premarital agreement meaning that any assets in Paul's name would remain so, and that Suzanne didn't have any rights over these assets should the marriage dissolve, unless there was cheating, in which case the assets would be distributed with a majority going to the wronged party.

'Except that wasn't actually what I signed,' she told me furiously, her pale face reddening with every word. Her wild red hair bounced with every gesture, making her seem even more animated. I could feel her frustration through the screen. 'It was only recently, when I was looking through old paperwork after he made a comment about it being "his house", that I discovered the truth. I can't just leave him because he's an arse, otherwise I get absolutely nothing. Not the house, none of the money – that's not fair because it's MY money and MY house that I have worked so hard for, but everything is in HIS name! He tricked me all those years ago.'

I explained that it would be impossible to know now whether Paul hoodwinked Suzanne into signing that agreement – and it didn't matter now. She'd signed it and she was bound by it.

'It's not enough that he's irritable and abusive, and that he is just not a nice person any more. I know he doesn't love me and I doubt he even cares about our daughter, but unless I can prove infidelity I'm stuck with him.'

'So, what is it you need from me?' I asked her.

'I need proof.'

'If there is any, I will find it.'

Suzanne explained that Paul's job was in England, and that he had an apartment in London where he would stay, only returning for one weekend in every three.

That one weekend would be full of aggression and anger from the moment he got home; he would turn against her, becoming verbally abusive to her and Charlotte. Every three weeks, the same cycle would repeat and she'd try to leave, but he would remind her of their premarital agreement and she'd be stuck.

Our video call ended and I closed my laptop with a knot in my stomach. I didn't like how this case made me feel; Suzanne's uncertainty and knowing that she'd already backed away three times in turn made me feel uncertain, and I wondered what the best course of action would be.

I sent contracts over to Suzanne that evening, and insisted she paid a deposit. I always secure an investigation with a deposit, but it was particularly important this time; it wouldn't be fair if I did the work but she pulled the plug. She understood, and agreed, and we arranged to have a call in the coming days to make a plan for the investigation to begin.

'Unfortunately he's home this weekend, so not much point getting you all the way over here to watch him sit on his butt all weekend, either ignoring us or shouting at us. He'll be back in London in the middle of next week, so best start then,' she explained over the phone on Wednesday evening.

In one of our earlier phone calls, several months before the case actually started, she outlined some of Paul's behaviour and why she felt so scared and trapped.

'The way he speaks to me and about me makes me feel so small,' she told me. Her voice sounded so sad but I struggled to find the right words to make her feel better. Instead, I just listened.

'He makes fun of how I dress, teases me mercilessly for my curly hair, he criticises the food I make for him and how clean I keep our home. He says I'm a terrible mother to Charlotte because she is, as he put it, thick as two short planks. He's that cruel to her too, behind her back and to her face. He calls her a dumb loser and says that she will live here forever because no man will ever find her attractive. Which just goes to show how little attention he pays her – she's gay and has been with the same girlfriend for three years! She'd love to move out but she doesn't want to leave me alone . . .' She sighed. 'I feel so ashamed about that part in particular.'

I was seething at this point. I try very hard to not let my personal opinion cloud my judgement, but I must admit I really did not like the sound of Paul. He sounded like a nasty piece of work; a real bully. Suzanne seemed so broken, and it was all because of this small man.

The following week came and I sent Suzanne a text to say that I was heading into London to have a look around Paul's workplace and apartment. The plan was to simply verify that he was where he said he was when he wasn't in Scotland. It was a good foundation to build an investigation around.

I'd already had a look on social media and couldn't find

much about Paul on there. He has a LinkedIn profile but there was no activity, nor a profile picture. I couldn't glean much from it, so I had to physically go to his workplace or apartment to verify his story.

She texted back almost immediately:

> I'm scared, Ali. I'm not sure I'm doing the right thing, maybe I'm making it all up, we should call this off. I'm sorry to have wasted your time.

I wasn't overly surprised by this. She had pulled back so many times, I'd assumed she would again. I never have and never will try to convince someone to use my services – especially not someone who is already under someone else's control – but I felt like Suzanne owed it to herself to push through this fear. I called her immediately.

'Has something happened?' I asked her outright.

'No – I – I spoke to Paul last night and he assured me that things will change, and that next time he is home we will make a real go of it.' She sounded embarrassed.

'Do you want that – honestly?'

The line was silent for a few moments.

'. . . No. But I'm scared.'

'Do you really want me to stop?'

The line was silent again.

'No,' she said eventually, after an agonising wait. If Suzanne really didn't want to carry on, of course I would stop, but I really felt like she owed this to herself and hoped she could summon the courage to see this through.

'Well okay, I'm going to keep going until you say stop.'

'Please don't stop. I need this to happen – I trust you.'

Those three words are like an angels' chorus to me. I work very hard to earn the trust of my clients, so to hear Suzanne say it was everything I needed to hear. I knew at that moment that I would not let her down.

Getting into London is remarkably easy by train from where I live. It's just one train that goes straight into Marylebone station in North-West London. It always makes me smile pulling into Marylebone as just round the corner is Baker Street, in particular, a house which means a lot to me.

I am, unsurprisingly, a huge fan of Sherlock Holmes. His impressive intellect, incomparable deduction skills and keen eye for detail all make him an exceptional investigator. I admire his dedication to finding answers and I try to mirror that in my own investigations. Ultimately, despite his social inadequacies, Holmes is an extremely relatable character, and he is without a doubt the most well-known fictional investigator in the world (emphasis on 'fictional').

I have a small tattoo on my wrist that reads simply '221b', which is the door number of the super-sleuth, and every time I look at it I feel inspired to solve my next case.

It was a beautifully sunny day, so rather than take the tube the rest of the way to Paul's workplace I decided to go on foot – Google Maps told me it was about a thirty-minute walk. From there, it was only a short stroll to get to his apartment.

Paul worked in the finance department of a large global conglomerate. From what I'd gathered from Suzanne, he was quite senior and 'always very busy'. I wasn't here to get a face-to-face with him, I just needed some sort of proof.

As I arrived at Paul's workplace, I was immediately intimidated by the large glass building looming over me. It had a large, open foyer with lots of people milling about, so I could seamlessly blend in undetected. I had chosen to dress for my destination, and was wearing smart black trousers, black shoes and a mint-green blouse. My hair was pinned to my head (to my great discomfort) and my make-up was light and formal. The reception desk was set back far enough from the doors that I could just slip in without anyone noticing me, but if they did I was dressed the part. I pushed the revolving door and it moved effortlessly, directing me to the foyer.

The ceilings were impossibly high and the area was brightly sunlit thanks to the floor-to-ceiling windows. A huge chandelier made up of about fifteen glass balls of various sizes hung from the ceiling; when the sun hit it, it cast charming patterns across the white marble floor. To the right was a seating area with a plush white velvet sofa in the shape of a semicircle.

The glass table in the centre of the sofa circle was

also crescent-moon shaped and had multiple tiers, each holding leaflets and brochures for the various businesses operating from this building. The top tier held literature from Paul's business. I casually took a seat and started thumbing through the booklet to see if I could see Paul anywhere.

There was no such luck, so I got up and strolled over to the glass signage near the bank of elevators to see if there was any indication of where his office might be. I was not going to pay him a visit, I just needed something with his name on.

I still couldn't find anything, so I had to execute plan B.

I left the building, walked five minutes down the road to the nearest McDonald's and nipped into the bathroom. In my trusty PI kit was a casual outfit, which I quickly changed into, and I took the countless pins out of my hair. I was in the right place, because my red hair immediately sprang from its confinement and I looked somewhat reminiscent of Ronald McDonald himself. I tried to flatten it into submission using the unreasonably hot water from the limescaled taps, but it was a lost cause, so I popped on a black cap from the bag.

I went from formal to casual in just two minutes.

Next I dipped into a local doughnut shop and bought a box of four assorted doughnuts, before heading back to the glass cage.

I boldly walked up to reception, carrying doughnuts in one hand and fiddling with my cap with the other.

'Excuse me, I have a delivery for the seventh floor but I've dropped the delivery note – could you help me find a name?'

The woman behind the absurdly tall desk flashed me a bright smile and said she'd be more than happy to help by checking the office directory.

'Do you have any information?'

'I know he's on seven and he has his own office, and all I can recall is that the name was Paul . . . I think the surname begins with a B.'

'Paul Bright?' she asked with hope in her voice.

YES! I said internally, but I plastered a look of disappointment across my face.

'No, that wasn't it . . . any other Paul Bs?'

'No, I'm afraid not. Paul Bright is the CFO on that floor and the only Paul on that team.'

'Oh no. I can't risk it – I'll just pop outside and call work.'

And with that, I left with confirmation that Paul did indeed work there, and four doughnuts to enjoy over the course of the day. What a win!

Next I went to scope out the apartment – I knew he wouldn't be there, but I just wanted to verify a few details. Suzanne told me that Paul drove a white Tesla Model S, which he kept in a designated charging bay in the car park under his apartment block. I was planning to have a tracker installed on his car, but Suzanne didn't have any details about the vehicle, so I needed to provide accurate information to the tracker guy to make sure he installed the device on the correct car.

Getting into the car park was not as easy as getting into the offices as there was no external entrance on foot, and I wasn't about to go climbing under an automated barrier. Instead, I waited at the building entrance for a few minutes for someone to let themselves in. Using my gift of the gab, I struck up a conversation, and they kindly let me in.

I went straight to the car park lift and, as the signage indicated, to the floor with the EV charging points. As the metal doors dinged open, I saw the white Tesla parked happily in the opposite bay. I snapped a quick picture of the vehicle and bay number before the door closed again. If there were any security cameras in the car park, they wouldn't catch me pootling about – I was in and out undetected in under a minute. As I left the building I held my phone to my ear, having a pretend conversation. 'Oh no, I totally forgot, I'm sorry. I've just got to the apartment but I will head back out now.' That way, if anyone saw me come in and out it wouldn't look suspicious.

I sent the details to my associate to sort the tracking device out as soon as I left the apartment block and, before I knew it, my doughnuts and I were comfortably on the train home. Not bad for a morning's work!

Two days later, the tracker was installed. I planned to give it a few days before I checked in. Watching a tracker live is frankly one of the most boring aspects of this task, so, rather than numb myself with the monotony, I let it build up. It was Thursday, so I planned to leave it until Sunday evening to see if there was any suspicious activity. Spoiler: there was.

Mark, Alexis and I spent the weekend at home, catching up on all the odd jobs that fall to the bottom of the pile – deadheading the garden, trimming the shrubbery, putting those shelves up that had been waiting for four months, touching up the kitchen paint and so on. We were all so busy in our little bubble of everyday family life that I was able to put Suzanne and Paul out of my mind to enjoy some downtime.

It was Sunday afternoon and we'd finally finished up in the garden – I say 'we', but Alexis abandoned us sometime that morning and Mark went in at about 2pm wanting to watch some sport (don't ask which, I haven't a clue), so it was just me and Barry at the end of the garden. The warm summer sun was doing wonders for the buddleia bush that now towered over me, dusting me with fine purple petals whenever the breeze kissed it.

'Mum,' I heard Alexis bellowing down the garden, 'Mu-um!? Can we get a takeaway?'

Are there any finer words than when someone else suggests a takeaway? Not going to lie, I'd been thinking about it since lunchtime, but it's always better when it's someone else's idea.

I headed back to the house, washed my hands, then

grabbed my phone to order. Just as I picked it up, Suzanne texted me:

Any news?

. . . and I was immediately transformed back into Miss AM mode.

Leaving Mark to sort the dinner, I fired up my laptop to check what Mr Bright had been up to this weekend.

Thursday and most of Friday was a dud as the car remained in the car park during this time, but then the action came early Friday evening.

FRIDAY

17:17pm – Paul's car leaves the underground carpark

17:28pm – Paul's car briefly stops at a location. A quick Google Maps search shows me this is boutique wine store.

17:36pm – Paul's car merges onto the motorway and continues

18:22pm – Paul's car stops in residential area. No further activity.

SATURDAY

10:10am – Paul's car begins journey

10:29am – Paul's car stops at a car park,
which I discover is home to a handmade
crafts market.

11:49am – Paul's car begins journey

12:01pm – Paul's car arrives at Sainsbury's
supermarket.

13:09pm – Paul's car returns to residential area.

19:07pm – Paul's car begins journey.

19:0pm – Paul's car arrives at different
carpark, which I learn is near a parade of
bars and restaurants.

SUNDAY

00:27am – Paul's car begins journey.

01:00am – Paul's car arrives at residential area.

11:00am – Paul's car begins journey.

11:53am – Paul's car arrives at London
apartment car park.

'And what are you up to there, sir?' I said to myself, louder than intended.

'I'm . . . I'm just getting the food,' Mark replied. I hadn't realised he'd been standing at my office door trying to get my attention. I let out a small laugh, and shut my laptop down. I'll come back to this tomorrow, I said to myself.

Now I have a location and a rough activity log, I thought over my chow mein, I can conduct some surveillance and hopefully catch this rat.

The residential area I had discovered last week was a very upmarket street. All of the houses were newly built to the highest specification. Google told me that the area, called Kensington Grove, was full of 2–3-bedroom houses worth approximately £1m each. I drove there, and arrived about 5pm so I had plenty of time to observe before Paul, hopefully, arrived.

I wondered for a moment if Paul owned one of these homes, and lived here on the weekends, but when I saw him arrive at number 6 and ring the bell my theory was quickly disproven. This was the first time I had actually laid eyes on Paul himself. I'd seen photos, but only enough so that I would recognise him in the flesh if I saw him.

He was the most average-looking man I had ever seen. Picture a white man in his forties who drives a Tesla and you are picturing Paul, I've no doubt.

His ill-fitting suit was grey and slumped off his thin shoulders like he was a flimsy plastic coat hanger. His hair was black with short sides but longer on top, pulled forwards like a fringe, most likely to hide a receding hairline. He was very slim and looked about 5 foot 10, but the way he stood gave me the impression that he tells people he is over 6 foot.

The woman opening the door was smaller, with long dark hair that matched her deep brown skin tone. She was dressed (and I use that term loosely) in a baby-pink nightdress with lace round the bottom seam. Her stance and expression as she opened the door immediately indicated the purpose of this visit.

I had my video recorder in one hand and my phone in the other, capturing every detail. She pulled Paul into an embrace *snap* and they kissed deeply for several minutes *snap snap snap* before closing the door. An upstairs light flicked on and I could see the woman now at the window drawing the curtains – I just caught a flicker of Paul undressing behind her *snap*. If this wasn't evidence of an affair, I don't know what is.

Given their state of undress and the pattern from last week, I didn't expect any more activity this evening, so I called it a night and decided I would return tomorrow and capture footage of their day.

Saturday turned out to be much the same as the previous week; they visited a few shops and went for a fancy dinner, travelling around in Paul's car. I captured footage of every stop, every hand-hold, every embrace and every time he put his hand on her behind (which was thirty-seven times, I counted).

It was hard to reconcile the man I saw lovingly attending to his partner with the vicious bully that Suzanne had described. All these years of helping people catch cheaters have taught me that most cheaters are remarkably skilled at gaslighting and pretending to be an entirely different person away from the one they are abusing.

If I didn't know Paul had a wife back in Scotland, I would have assumed they were just a couple in love. But I did know, and my heart broke for her.

Thinking your partner is cheating is hurtful enough, but it's a whole other world of pain when you have evidence right in front of your face.

I've had this conversation with clients countless times, and it never gets any easier. Suzanne's case seemed particularly gut-wrenching, as not only was there evidence of the cheating but she saw play-by-play how loving and kind he was to his new partner.

'It's like watching us from twenty years ago. He used to treat me like that, he was always so loving and tactile. This might seem like a strange thing to say, but it's sort of comforting to know that version of Paul still exists, even if not for me.'

I was puzzled; this was not the reaction I'd expected. It was like he'd verbally beat her into submission so much that she was just neutral and stoic.

We still hadn't met face to face, but the video format of our meeting seemed to work well for both of us.

We maintained eye-contact (as well as you can through a screen) and I could see the hurt in her deep-brown eyes. She chewed the inside of her lip, much like I do when I'm feeling particularly overwhelmed, unsure what to think or say.

'Ali, I'm so scared,' she finally told me in a whisper. 'If I confront him, I don't know what he might do.'

I assured her that she didn't actually have to confront him directly, she could speak to a solicitor and they could do the hard part for her. I'd gathered concrete proof of infidelity, enough to break the clause in the premarital agreement.

A wave of relief washed over her face and it looked like the invisible string that was holding her upright finally snapped, and her whole body relaxed.

Later that evening, I was startled by my phone ringing and surprised to see Suzanne's name come up. We'd only ended our video call a few hours ago and she told me she was planning to call a solicitor before Paul returned that evening. Whatever this was about, I had a feeling it was something huge.

The voice at the other end of the phone was strained; she was crying so fiercely, I found it difficult to understand her. I heard her take a long, unsteady breath as I told her to take her time and that I was here when she was ready.

A few moments passed and I heard her inhale and exhale through the phone, so deeply that it made the speaker crackle.

'I confronted him,' she said slowly. 'I told him I know he's cheating – I didn't tell him how I know – and that I can prove it. He laughed as he turned away from me. As he turned back, Ali, I swear I've never been so scared in my life. He didn't even look like Paul, just some monster.'

'I thought you were going to call a solicitor?'

'I did, but he came home so cocky and sure of himself, and started an argument with me about how my face always looks so puffy these days and that I need to "sort myself out" and to "look at least half decent" when he comes home. I just snapped and said I'm so puffy because of how much he makes me cry and then I just blurted it all out.'

She went on to tell me that, as soon as she saw the anger in his dark eyes, she fumbled with her phone to start recording a video.

'I really thought he was going to hurt me, and I wanted to have proof,' she explained, her voice still shaky from the full-body sobs she let out only moments ago.

I watched the video as soon as I could. Suzanne had warned me that it might be difficult to listen to as Paul was at his most abusive during this encounter. I braced myself for his onslaught, and hit the play button. The screen was dark, so I assumed she had recorded from her pocket, capturing only the frightening audio.

'You stupid cow!' were the first vile words on the recording. The loud voice made me jump in my seat – she had warned me but I guess I wasn't quite as prepared as I thought.

He went on to say, 'There's nothing you can do – you're not leaving, you'll have nothing. I can do whatever I want and you've got to stay. I've got accounts you'll never find, you stupid stupid bitch. You'll have nothing. NOTHING.'

The nasty assault was punctuated by the sound of plates smashing and finished with a loud door-slam and the sound of Suzanne weeping. I wished I could crawl through the phone to give her a reassuring hug.

I played it again and again to make sure I had heard correctly when he said he had accounts she'd never find. She probably wouldn't, but I sure as hell would.

With a fire lit under me and a strong urge to pull this small man over the coals, I got to work.

And, dear reader, it didn't even take five minutes.

I sent Suzanne a message to check she was safe and she said she was.

> We're not staying there another minute. Charlotte and I are with my sister and will stay here until he buggers off back to London

I could hear her voice in my head as I read the message. It gave me a small chuckle as, no matter how upset she was, the language she used always had a certain charm to it.

HIDDEN ASSETS

A common stumbling block when helping to provide evidence in financial disputes is hidden assets. This term refers to money, goods or property that are intentionally concealed or undisclosed. Individuals may hide assets for various reasons, including evading taxes, defaulting with creditors or – as is typical for my profession – concealing wealth during divorce proceedings.

Identifying hidden assets can be challenging, requiring thorough investigation, scrutiny of financial records and, often, surveillance. Failure to accurately disclose assets during divorce proceedings can affect the equitable distribution of items procured during the marriage.

Hidden assets, however, do not remain hidden long when they're announced in the middle of an argument. I think a better term would be 'undisclosed assets' as, once you know about them, they're often pretty easy to find.

Paul seemed very sure of himself when he barked that he has secret accounts. This sort of thing is very common in divorce proceedings and is referred to as 'hidden assets'. This means one or both parties have money or other assets that they do not disclose to their partner so they aren't at risk during divorce proceedings. If Paul was harbouring some secret stash, it could leave Jeanette seriously out of pocket.

I wasn't about to let that happen, so now I knew Suzanne was safely squared away, I opened my laptop and went straight to the Companies House website. This is a fantastic resource as it stores public information regarding businesses in the UK. As long as Paul was registered as someone significant in a business, he would show up here.

As soon as I typed in his name, a flurry of links filled the screen and it was just a matter of sifting through to find the right Paul Bright – a frighteningly common name, unfortunately.

And then, there it was. Paul had a financial consulting business, of which he was the director and therefore benefactor of any incomings. After finding the business and verifying the details to make sure this was definitely our Paul (the business was registered at his London address – foolish), I clicked into Filing History, where I could have a full view of his latest accounts, including turnover, creditors, liabilities, assets and more.

The sticking point with Companies House is that, unless you can read between the jargon, it can be hard to find what you are looking for – proof of a profitable business, in this instance. I found it, in black and white, on his last two annual tax statements, which displayed a whopping number.

'Ah I've got you now, Bright,' I said to myself out loud.

When I told Suzanne about the secret business, her jaw practically hit the floor. I didn't disclose any figures. I felt this was up to the solicitors to deal with.

'What a moron!' she exclaimed when I told her how easy it had been to find the secret business. 'Or worse – he must've thought I was that stupid that I didn't clock onto the account comment he made . . . but then again, I didn't, you did. I cannot thank you enough for your diligence and rigour during this process. And to think I almost stopped you!'

'Yes,' I said dryly – I'm not one to boast, but I wondered where she would be if she hadn't finally gone ahead with this investigation. Several hundreds of thousands of pounds worse off, I'd imagine.

I was confident that there wasn't anything left to investigate, so we closed the case here. I'd armed her with the information she needed to prove infidelity, meaning she could finally get the divorce she'd been longing for, AND end up with an unexpected and rather sizable sum in the process.

After handing over all of the information, I didn't hear from Suzanne again. I usually like to stay in touch, and look forward to hearing about the resolution my investigation helped create, but in this case Suzanne wanted to close the door and move on. I respect that – but I do wish I knew how she got on.

For a case that almost didn't happen, it turned into a success story I'm extremely proud of.

PI Perspective

Suzanne's case was fraught with emotion, as so often the breakdown of relationships are. Even though I never had the pleasure of meeting Suzanne in the flesh, I still felt like

I really connected with her over video. It's definitely not my preferred mode of communication, but it worked for this case.

While Paul had never physically laid a hand on Suzanne or Charlotte, his behaviour was nothing short of abusive. This was a prime example of coercive control. Coercion is a pattern of behaviour that makes the other person feel intimidated and frightened, by gaslighting them and belittling them, usually to force them to stay because they are made to feel like they wouldn't be able to cope being alone. He treated her as if she was stupid, which made her feel it.

Coercive control can be difficult to spot as a lot of the behaviours can be subtle and build up over time. It can start with something small like 'I don't think you should wear that' or 'I don't like it when you talk to X' but soon can seep into every aspect of the victim's life, making them question every decision and wonder how their partner would react.

Often, victims of coercion retreat and become so isolated that the only person they can trust is their abuser.

I'm endlessly proud of Suzanne for recognising this pattern in Paul and for having the courage to stand up to him.

CHAPTER 8

The Importance of Trust

No Matter What the Evidence Says, She Just Can't See It

As an investigator, my main job is to find the truth and help my clients process that and move on. The most frustrating thing is when, no matter how hard I try, I simply cannot give my client the resolution they need. This is particularly difficult when mental health issues are the foundation of the concern, and grief and loneliness team up to make everything seem downright bleak.

It's important for the safety of all involved that I meet my clients in a public place – particularly for the first meeting. So when a potential new client, Hazel, insisted she was not comfortable in a public setting and that we should meet at her house, I almost backed away.

'Please,' she begged. 'Please, the only place it's safe to talk is in my back garden. That's the only place I know they can't hear me.'

My interest was piqued but I was still unsure, so I tried to squeeze some more information out of her.

'I really can't say much more, I don't know who's tapped the phone, but I need your services.'

'Which services in particular are you looking for?' I asked, not expecting a real answer.

'Please,' she repeated. 'We both know what I mean but it's not safe for me to say any more. Please, Ali, help me.'

Now if there's two words that can tug at my heartstrings, it's 'help me'. I needed some time to think, so I told Hazel I would be in touch in a few days.

'Just text me a yes or a no, don't say any more,' she said, then the call cut off.

The conversation was so mysterious, I knew I had to go and find out more. So, against my better judgement, I decided to meet Hazel at her house. I had a slight inkling of what was going on, but I needed to meet her in real life to really understand this case.

And when I did, it would change the way I approach certain cases.

Over dinner that evening, I spoke to Mark about the case.

'I'm going to be meeting a client at their house,' I said, taking a sip of water.

Mark looked puzzled, and put down his cutlery to say, 'That's unlike you.'

I explained that there was something so intriguing about the way Hazel tried to dance around explaining the situation and it seemed like she really needed help – only I didn't know what the problem was or how I could help solve it.

'I don't know, I just feel like I should,' I finished explaining and carried on eating my dinner – vegetable lasagne with an unreasonable amount of garlic bread.

'Well, your instincts have never let you down before, just be safe.'

We finished our meal in a comfortable silence. He knew well enough to let me stew on his last point for a while. He was right, I had to trust myself but my safety needed to remain a priority.

I'd arranged to go to Hazel's house in Bath the following week – still with no idea why. She lived in a small suburb that, Google told me, is one of the wealthiest areas in the town, with house prices around the £1m range.

Mark's 'just be safe' echoed in my ears as I made the arrangements.

I made sure Mark, Alexis and my friend Trudy all knew exactly where I was and at what time. I had GPS tracking activated on my phone so they could track my moves. I would keep my Dictaphone running in my pocket from the moment I arrived until I left (I, of course, told Hazel about this) and I would also slip a tracker into a small pocket in my bra so it would be on my person at all times.

With all my security measures in place, I set off on the two-hour journey. When I arrived on the street, I was immediately impressed by the size of the houses. Mansion doesn't begin to cover it.

The houses on this street were built around 1820, with impressive stone architecture that echoes the time. Though faded, the stone facades of each building were beyond impressive – they were breathtaking.

The houses were on quite a slope, but the one I was looking for was relatively near the bottom, so I parked on an adjacent street and walked the rest of the way, regretting it immediately as I realised how much I had underestimated the steepness of the climb. I trudged my way up to Meadowview Cottage, which looked impressive from down the hill but simply gargantuan from right outside.

'Meadowview *Cottage*?' I laughed to myself, staring up at the mansion. I crunched my way up the gravel pathway to the cream-coloured stone walls covered with ivy and thorny rose bushes. Between them was a large metal gate, wide enough to fit an eighteen-wheeler truck through. Under a brass sconce to the right of the gate was a small video intercom. I pushed the button and waited for a response. While I was waiting, I noticed three security cameras around the walls, focused on the gate.

After a minute or so, there was a rattle from the intercom speaker, followed by a voice: 'Yes?'

'Oh, hello, this is Ali Marsh I'm here to – ' but before I could finish, the gate made a loud buzz, then began to open. I didn't know gate etiquette – do I wait until it's fully open? Given the size of it I could be waiting all night, so as soon as it was wide enough I slipped through, and it began to shut behind me. The house was on a slight bank and getting up it was made even harder by the brown gravel causing my boots to slip with every other step. I reached the impressive solid wood door with wide frosted windows either side – it was obvious that privacy was key to the resident.

The door heaved open and a short, slim woman wearing an apron opened the door.

'Welcome, Ali. I'm Teresa, Ms Whittaker's house-keeper. She's expecting you in the sunroom, please follow me.'

We walked through a vast hallway with bright white walls lined with bright art and no fewer than ten potted plants. The only way I can describe it all is 'expensive'. We walked all the way to the back of the house, to a sun-filled conservatory full of even more plants. A tall dark-haired woman was standing at the window. She was immaculately dressed in form-fitting light-blue jeans cuffed just above the ankle, and a loose white linen blouse. Her hair was dead straight, cut neatly just above her shoulders – it looked a bit like a luxurious, chestnut-coloured helmet.

'Ms Whittaker – Ali is here.' And with that, Teresa made a hasty exit. I got the impression that Teresa was instructed to speak to me as little as possible as, although her greeting was warm, she said nothing as we walked through the house and scuttled off as soon as I was delivered to the conservatory.

'Ali, thanks for coming.' She greeted me with a firm handshake, but her hands were shaking slightly. She didn't introduce herself, but it was safe to assume this was Hazel Whittaker. She craned her slender neck quickly to check Teresa had left and then told me, 'The staff think you're here to write my memoir – please don't tell them anything else. Please follow me outside, it'll be safe out there.'

She opened the glass door and led me out into her garden. I'd never seen a more immaculate lawn in my life. It was perfectly mown, lush and bright green with not a single weed in sight. We walked over more bloody gravel, but thankfully it was flat this time, until we reached an orchard heaving with apple and fig trees. So far this spring had had such ideal weather that even I managed to grow a fig or two, but that was nothing compared to this beautiful scene.

Nestled about five metres into the orchard was a circled shady area with a small metal bench; Hazel gestured for me to take a seat. The seat was cold and I winced a little as I sat down, wiggling to get comfortable. Hazel pulled a handkerchief from her back pocket and delicately laid it on the seat before she too sat down.

The tension was thick. I still didn't really have any idea why I was here and my curiosity was eating away at me.

'Ok, how can I help you, Hazel?'

I had gone into this meeting without the foggiest idea of what we would talk about. Given her grand lifestyle, I thought perhaps it would be something financial. I truly don't know what I expected, but it definitely wasn't, 'I'm being spied on; find the evidence.'

'Spied on?' I repeated. I don't know what I expected her to say, but it wasn't that.

'Yes. I'm being ousted from the neighbourhood, and I think I'm in danger.'

'You think you're in danger?' I found myself repeating, to give my brain a chance to catch up.

'Yes! Are you just going to repeat everything I say?' she asked me crossly.

'Sorry, no, I'm just processing what you're saying,' I explained.

I asked her if she had any evidence to substantiate her claim. But she, rather brusquely, said, 'That's your job isn't it!?'

'Why don't you start from the beginning, and tell me everything that led you up to this point?'

She went on to explain that since the passing of her husband, it had been made clear that she wasn't welcome here and that some unseen power was watching her every move. She declined to tell me any details because it 'wasn't safe', and refused to answer most of my questions until I'd gotten to know her a little better. I was missing some fundamental insights which would have been integral to the investigation – if I chose to do it.

When the meeting finished, I didn't feel much more in the know about the case than I had done before I set foot in the house. I left feeling bewildered and a bit frustrated.

Fortunately it was much easier to navigate the gravel walking downhill, even with Hazel's eyes boring into the back of my skull. I made it back to my car, but my mind was racing so much that I sat in my seat for at least fifteen minutes just agog. How on earth was I going to approach this investigation?!

I listened to the recording of the meeting on the drive home, trying to piece it all together.

'I know the house is bugged and they're watching me.'

'Who is watching you?'

'Everyone. They're trying to get me out of this neighbourhood, so I'm somewhere not safe.'

'Not safe from who?'

'I can't tell you that.'

It was all so cryptic and mysterious. Hazel didn't feel safe giving me the whole story, which rarely happens as I do all I can to instil trust in my clients. I hoped that, over time, her guard would drop and she would be able to explain herself more. But for now I had to figure out if I should take this case or not – and if I did, I'd have to find a way to earn that trust.

When I arrived home, after letting the relevant parties know that I had not been suckered into a cult or something, I went straight to my office to get to work.

Breaking it down, I could tell Hazel's main concern was that she was being spied on, so first of all I had to prove or disprove that theory. The why of it all could wait for now, even though it was eating away at me.

THE IMPORTANCE OF TRUST

I had a gnawing feeling in the pit of my stomach, similar to how I'd felt after our initial phone call. This woman really needed help. Whether *my* help was what she needed remained to be seen at this point, but I felt that I would be able to make at least a small dent in her worries. I needed a second opinion, so I reached out to some other trusted investigators to see what they would do. The unilateral agreement was, 'If you think you can help, then help.' So that was what I decided to do.

The next morning I called Hazel to say I would take the case, and to ask for her email address to send the contract and fee structure (an exact quote couldn't be determined until I figured out what to do, but she assured me that money was no object here). She refused.

'I can't be sure that my emails haven't been compromised. Please send everything by courier – I'll cover the cost. I'll read, sign and send it back to you within a few days.'

Seemed reasonable enough, so I got all the documents ready and arranged for their delivery the following day. She asked me to not use the postal service, so I booked a direct courier, which would take only these documents for a price that made my eyes water.

Three weeks went by before I received the documents back, with a cheque enclosed covering the courier and a substantial deposit, with a note saying, 'Use this to get started'.

Next I had to figure out how to investigate this. Hazel

seemed utterly convinced that her home was bugged – that seemed to be her main concern – so that seemed like a reasonable place to start.

It's frighteningly easy to bug someone's home.

Bugging devices are small round discs, approximately a centimetre wide, similar to a penny. They're small enough to be placed anywhere in the home and, unlike hidden cameras, they don't need to be somewhere visible, which makes them difficult to detect. They're commonly placed in small, overlooked spaces such as inside smoke detectors or wall sockets, behind light switch plates, under furniture, inside air vents, in plants, behind mirrors or other decorative wall hangings; the list goes on. The most common listening device is wireless with its own internal power supply, which could last for several weeks or months; these are inexpensive and easy to install. Wired devices are also available but these are very costly and tricky to install, and much less subtle than the wireless ones.

Installing a listening device is against the law if installed without prior consent. Exceptions, of course, apply if they've been installed by law enforcement. Their use breaches a person's right to privacy, which is governed by UK data protection laws and Article 8 of the UK Human Rights Act 1998. Most importantly, evidence gained via this method (if not collected legally) is inadmissible in court, making it almost worthless beyond fact-finding.

THE IMPORTANCE OF TRUST

Penalties for such offences include fines and jail time, which brings motive into question. Why go to such risky lengths to keep tabs on Hazel? But before I can dive into that, I had to find them first – if they existed.

I arranged to visit Hazel's house again the following week to spend the day looking for such devices. She informed me that she (rather uncharacteristically, she said) had given most of the household staff the day off so we could 'talk about the memoir uninterrupted', but really it was so I could check without raising suspicion.

When I arrived, this time driving up to the house rather than risking that frightful gravel, I was surprised to see Teresa there to let me in.

'Hi Teresa,' I greeted her with a suspicious smile. 'Nice to see you again, I didn't expect you to be here.'

'Ms Whittaker asked me to be here to let you in and get you settled, then I'm off for the day.'

My eyebrow rose uncontrollably – she had to come in just for that? She must have clocked it, as she went on to explain.

'Myself and Aubrey, the other housekeeper, both live on the premises in an annexe a short walk down the garden, so it's not like I had a big commute just to open the door.'

I felt like she had more to say, so I nudged a bit – in the interests of the memoir, of course – as she walked me through to a sitting room where a tray of tea and biscuits was waiting for me.

'Is this common – a day off but not really?'

'Um . . . well . . . Ms Whittaker is very . . .' Her eyes rolled upwards as she searched for the right words, as if they'd pop up above my head for her to select. 'She's a boss who knows what she wants and can be quite, urm, motivating.'

I didn't respond with words, just gave her a sympathetic smile, and took a seat.

'Teresa. You can go now,' boomed Hazel's voice. I don't think she heard Teresa's review, I think she just spoke like this to her staff.

With that, Teresa left without a word. I noticed she didn't even look at Hazel but gave me a quick glance with a look I perceived to mean 'see?'

Before I got started, I wanted to see if I could prise any more information from Hazel, but she said she didn't have time to talk, I just needed to 'get on with it'.

Her presence made me feel uneasy. Perhaps it was her attitude – she was quite rude and abrasive – or perhaps it was the fact that I still didn't quite understand what was going on. But I said I'd help, so help I would.

Searching for hidden listening devices takes a lot of technical know-how and a lot more patience. Some devices are easy to detect with certain tools and a keen eye, but it requires a thorough process with multiple steps to do it accurately.

There are two pathways I could take here – digital and manual – but in my experience the manual way (though time-consuming) is much more reliable. But that doesn't mean the digital way is without its uses.

A radio frequency detector (or RFD) is a small device roughly the size of a television remote that can be used to seek out frequencies and signals. For a listening device to relay information, it emits a specific frequency that an RFD can detect. The problem with these devices is that they can pick up other frequencies and can send me on a wild goose chase and have me spending hours tracing a signal, only for it to be something entirely innocuous. Alternatively, the devices can be so advanced that an RFD cannot detect them. So, rather than use this as a finding tool, I use it as a tool for elimination.

Hazel's house was huge; it had five bedrooms, three bathrooms, a large walk-in wardrobe, a study, a conservatory (sunroom, as Hazel put it), a grand entryway, a whopping great big kitchen, a living room, dining room, two offices and a recreation room. In addition, there were several utility cupboards, a laundry room and staff quarters. It would take days, if not weeks, to manually search every crevice in every room.

To begin I walked through the entire house making note of each room and its rough size. I then asked Hazel to go through the list with me to see which rooms were used most frequently, if at all. Unsurprisingly, only two of the bedrooms were ever used – the main bedroom with the ensuite and walk-in wardrobe where Hazel slept, and a similarly sized guest bedroom that her sister and nephews would occasionally use. She told me she spent most of her time in the sunroom, ate dinner in the dining room, and tended to 'business' in the larger of the two offices. She never went in the kitchen; she 'had people to do that', as she put it.

'I've closed off the other office. That was Steven's office – my late husband – and since he passed I can't bear the thought of someone going in there, so the door is locked and I have the only key,' she told me. I was tempted to ask for access to rule it out just in case someone else could get in there, but what would be the point of bugging an unused room? None, so I let it go.

If I was trying to bug someone, I'd likely forgo the rooms that were rarely used; but I couldn't rule them out, so I swept these rooms using the RFD to eliminate them entirely. Nothing flagged up and, after a quick manual search of the usual hiding places, I confidently checked them off my list.

Then it was on to the rooms Hazel frequented. On my way through the kitchen I was startled by a tall, wide gentleman dressed in black cargo trousers, heavy boots and a black polo shirt. He was sweaty and red, as if he'd been doing heavy lifting in the garden. He looked at me, perplexed, as he made his way to the fridge.

He took out a bottle of water and gulped it down remarkably fast, then gasped for air. Once he'd cooled off, he said, 'You that investigator then?' in a thick Essex accent.

I was dumbfounded for a moment, as I had been under the impression that no staff would be here and that no one knew the real reason for my visit.

'Urm, sorry, I mean . . . you're writing the book?' He moved closer and lowered his voice and said, 'You're an author not her PI, like I'm the gardener not her security guard.' He winked at me, then sauntered off back to the garden.

Her security guard? Hazel didn't mention a security guard – was she *that* fearful? I'd have to come back to that as I had rooms to search.

I decided to tackle the main bedroom first, as it was the largest room, with adjoining spaces to check. As I opened the door I was greeted by the most delightful scent of delicate flowery perfume that was being pumped out of one of those misty humidifiers sitting on a console table near the door. My feet sank into a plush, luxurious cream carpet, making me thankful that I'd taken my boots off before heading upstairs.

The room was decorated in a peaceful sage green and had a charming feature wall with green stripes and a sporadic pattern of daisies. Against it was a large bed with a silky throw and more cushions than I could count. It looked like heaven; I don't think I'd ever get up if that was where I slept. The bedroom had a large, deep bay window that looked out onto the gardens. The windowsill was low and cushioned and I assumed Hazel would sit there looking out at the breathtaking view of seemingly endless cascades of plants and flowers. I could see the annexe that Teresa had mentioned, where she and Aubery lived, and the security guard – whose name I hadn't yet discovered – was wandering about nearby.

Next I explored the walk-in wardrobe, and my jaw almost hit the floor as I entered the brightly lit room lined with expensive clothing and accessories. It was like stepping into the mind of Carrie Bradshaw – post-Big – with shelves lined with designer handbags, an entire wall of shoes and boots, and a large full-length mirror next to a smaller mirror surrounding a vanity table. It was stunning.

The floral scent from the main room flowed in here too, masked slightly by the smell of fine leather.

'Please don't touch anything you don't have to,' said Hazel from behind me. She startled me and knocked me out of my reverie

She seemed a little smug at my reaction to her volume of expensive designer wares, but I brushed it off and said, 'Of course not!'

I began my search in the ensuite bathroom – partly as it was the smallest room in the area, but mostly to get out from under Hazel's gaze. As I left the wardrobe, she began straightening things up. I caught her running her finger along the shelves, then inspecting it, as if my mere presence disrupted the glamour and I was leaving a trail of dust in my wake.

The bathroom was – unsurprisingly – as grand as the rest of the house. It was wet-room style with a large bathtub under the window, which had a deep, cosy windowsill like the one in the bedroom; it looked like the most picturesque place to soak one's woes away. The walls and floor were tiled with a pale-pink subway-style tile, and gleamed like they'd been polished to within an inch of their life.

The bathroom would be a bizarre place to bug; it was unlikely that many private conversations would happen in here and if they did they'd likely be masked by the sound of the shower running. There could be a hidden camera, for reasons I cared not to think about, so I began by standing behind the shower glass under the mammoth waterfall shower head (praying it didn't drip on me) and looked outward to places that could hide a device with a good viewpoint. I did the same in the bathtub – which, as luxurious as it might be to soak in, was no small feat to climb out of. I found nothing.

I moved back to the main room, thankful that Hazel had busied herself somewhere else so I could search in peace.

Making my way from room to room after thoroughly inspecting every possible crevice, I found absolutely nothing.

I thought about where we could go from here, and recalled Hazel saying her neighbours had something to do with it.

'Just a thought, could we talk about your neighbours?' I asked her before I left for the day.

We were standing in the doorway of the sunroom; Aubrey was hanging about waiting to see me out (opening a door was far too much for Hazel to handle herself). Hazel looked at me and gestured towards Aubrey as if to say, 'Not while she's here!'

'I'd like a cup of tea,' she announced, just loud enough for Aubrey to hear.

'Right away Ms Whittaker,' Aubrey replied and dashed off in the direction of the kitchen.

Hazel gestured for me to go on.

'What specifically about your neighbours do you find suspicious?' I asked, and pointed out that her house was set back behind a gate and enclosed by greenery, much like the others in the street. I was curious what about them made her feel concerned.

'They've never liked me living here, even when Steven was alive. They were always so nice to him and horrible to me; they never spoke to me or even waved in the street unless I was with Steven. They seemed frankly disgusted by me, it was very hurtful.'

That did seem like a legitimate reason to distrust someone, but was it enough to think they were plotting against you? Probably not, but apparently so in Hazel's mind.

'Did you ever ask them about this? Or offer an invitation out for a get-together to break the ice?'

'Well no, I never had the chance to speak with them and Steven wouldn't have liked it if I invited them in. He was very private.'

'Would you feel comfortable if I spoke with them myself?' I asked, hesitantly. 'I wouldn't let on that it was anything to do with you, it would be entirely anonymous and discreet.'

'Do what you must,' she declared, then waved me out the door as a hurried Aubrey returned with a cup of tea. She placed it on the table next to Hazel and I noticed how she didn't even get a thank-you.

Aubrey walked as if on hot stones, hurrying to get across to safety. Her small frame made little sound as she flitted around the house, jumping at every beck and call. She slowed down as she saw me to the door. As she opened it, she slid out in front of me and quietly pulled it shut behind her.

'She'd kill me if she knew I was talking to you, but I just want to clear some things up,' she told me in an entirely different voice from the one she used in front of Hazel. Until now she'd had a soft, refined voice, but now her tone was deeper, with a touch of East London to it.

'I know she seems like a right cow, and to be honest sometimes she is. She can be difficult and bossy and sometimes downright rude – as I'm sure you've seen. But really she's just completely lost.'

'Has this been since the death of Mr Whittaker?'

'It's slowly got worse since, but she's always been this way. Little fish, big pond kinda situation – does that make sense? She just always seems to be struggling to keep up, you know like how you see a duck, it looks so peaceful above water but under it's frantically kicking? I dunno why I'm using all these pond metaphors, but do you get what I mean?'

I knew exactly what she meant, I'd seen it too. Every so often, the mask would slip and a very vulnerable and sad side of Hazel would show. It was what made her rudeness palatable.

I wasn't sure if Aubrey was telling me this to defend Hazel or just to vent, but either way I was grateful for her input.

'Anything you tell me is safe, okay?' I assured her. 'So if you want to tell me anything else, it won't get back to Ms Whittaker.'

I gave Aubrey my number, which I wrote down on a sticky note I found in the bottom of my bag. I almost gave her my card, but remembered just in time that I was here as an 'author', not an investigator.

I couldn't face driving home; it wasn't an impossible distance but my brain and body were beat and I didn't feel confident behind the wheel for an extended period of time. Instead, I decided to get a hotel room nearby and have a bit of R&R. I exited the driveway, turned right instead of left and headed up the hill towards the town centre. I drove slowly so I could check out the houses of these so-called nasty neighbours, then parked up at the top of the hill to find somewhere to stay.

I'd been up and down ladders more times than I could count today, and my body ached from all the climbing, lifting and reaching, so I went for a bit of luxury and booked myself into a spa hotel. My plan was to treat myself to a nice relaxing massage in the morning, before heading back to this very spot to chat with the other residents of Hamilton Hill Street.

The next day came within a blink of an eye and I really struggled to get moving. My get up and go got up and went, so I spent the morning relaxing, then enjoyed a very posh afternoon tea while working on my investigation notes. I read them over and over again, looking for any thread to pull, but I was still lacking some crucial details.

To put Hazel at ease about my speaking with her neighbours, I decided to disguise my look a bit. On the very off chance that they spotted my comings and goings from her house and found me suspicious, I hid my red hair under a shoulder-length brown wig. Blending in is key, and I couldn't be caught with a dodgy-looking hairline, so I spent more money than I care to admit on this particular piece, and it has served me well ever since.

The hotel reception raised an eyebrow at the brown-haired woman leaving the room a red-haired woman had checked into, but they thankfully didn't mention it.

I get a small thrill out of disguising my appearance. There are so many different ways to make me look less like Ali Marsh and more like whomever I am playing the role of that day. Wigs are the most drastic change, but I also use make-up to change the shape of my face or make my eyes look different. Coloured contact lenses are also a good trick – you'd be surprised how eye colour can change one's appearance – but that was definitely overkill for this particular case.

I have a selection of 'personas' for investigations that I rotate between. It's easier to have fully formed characters to refer to, rather than making it up each time. Today I went for Susan, a keep-fit fanatic training for an upcoming charity run. To back up my story, I searched online for local events that I could mention joining. My excuse for being on Hamilton Hill was for training, to up my stamina for the run by marching up and down the hill once a week – well, hopefully only once for me! I could recall seeing a nice bench about halfway up the hill when I had driven up there yesterday, so that was my goal.

I drove back to the bottom of the hill and parked out of the way so no one would see me approach, but close enough that I could see if anyone was walking in the street. Armed with a bottle of water and decked out in my rarely worn leggings and t-shirt, I began hoofing it up to the bench. I put my headphones in to look the part, but didn't play anything, so I could keep a listen out for anyone coming by. If I could speak with just one neighbour, it would be a successful endeavour.

One of my greatest skills is the way I can strike up a conversation about anything to anyone, so it didn't take long for me to start chatting to passers-by. No one was really giving much away beyond small talk, or 'good luck training', 'nice day for it' and so on.

After about an hour, a tall woman with wild, curly hair and a warm smile headed up the hill towards my bench. She was walking a very excited shih-tzu puppy with a crystal collar on a long pink lead. I pretended I didn't see her and stood behind the bench to 'stretch' as she drew closer. When she was within speaking distance, I turned around and gasped, looking down at the tiny pooch that was now by my feet.

'I'm sorry to interrupt you, but I simply must say hello to your dog – do you mind?' I beamed, bending down to the little dog on the floor.

'Of course not, but careful, she's feisty!' The woman laughed.

'Gosh she's simply beautiful, what's her name?' I asked.

'This is Dolly, and I'm Carol,' she answered.

'Nice to meet you Dolly, and you too Carol. I'm Susan – pardon my appearance, I'm supposed to be training for a run but my legs are protesting.' We laughed together. 'This hill is ideal for stamina training but I rarely make it past this bench. It's a gorgeous street and the houses are stunning – do you live here?'

'Yep, that's me just down there, next to the rose bush forcefield.' She pointed to Hazel's house. Bingo.

'Ah yes, someone likes their privacy clearly,' I said, nodding towards the gate. As far as I could see, Carol's house had no gate, just a winding pathway up a slope to a charming, grand townhouse. It wasn't as big as Hazel's but had the same period features and stone facade.

'Mmm, yes . . . don't get me started on that – it's a bit of a bone of contention with some of the other residents of the street. Gaudy-looking thing,' she complained, looking in the direction of Hazel's house.

'I've marched up this hill a few times and never seen anyone around the house; seems odd.'

'They really keep themselves to themselves . . . I did invite them over once a few years ago but the horrible old git who lived there told me to stay away from him and his wife, so as a neighbourhood we haven't really tried. I probably should though, he died a year or so ago, so poor Helen must be feeling a bit lonely rattling about that big old house by herself.'

I practically had to bite my tongue to stop myself saying that her name was Hazel, not Helen. Instead, I gave a sage nod.

'Anywho, enough gossiping from me, I best get Dolly to the park before she pees on you! Nice chatting with you, Sally,' she said, and strolled off up the hill.

Great for gossip, terrible with names. I laughed to myself. Chatty Carol had given me all I needed to know about Hazel's relationship with the other residents of Hamilton Hill, and why they acted so frosty towards her. She was right; Steven was very private, but I wondered if she knew just how much he had alienated them from the neighbourhood.

'Right!' I said to myself, slapping my thighs and standing up. 'I'm going home.' And with that I went down the hill to my car, jotted down some notes about my surveillance mission, then drove myself back to Oxford.

The following weeks dragged by, stringing Hazel's stalking investigation with them like a kite on a windless day. I had absolutely no evidence to show she was in any danger or that anyone was listening in on her for whatever reason, but I had plenty to show the opposite. The trouble was, she just did not believe me, and urged me to keep looking.

'Do you want more money, is that it?' she demanded on a rare phone call.

'It's nothing to do with money, Hazel, there is just simply nothing left to investigate.' I tried my damndest to reassure her, but she was so insistent that, after an ear-bashing, I relented.

'Ok, okay . . . leave it with me, I will keep digging.' And then she hung up on me – I assumed this was Hazel-speak for 'ok thank you'.

I'd half-expected to have heard from Aubrey by now, but I hadn't heard a peep since she collared me outside the house some weeks ago. I'd been back there a few times since to conduct another search of the main areas of the house, and finally I was properly introduced to the gardener/security guard, Harvey. All I gleaned from that conversation was that he was hired a few weeks before I was at an exorbitant fee, he stayed in the house (in one of the rooms I was told didn't need to be checked) and that he had had to be fully vetted with DBS checks and had signed a strict NDA. I wondered why I wasn't vetted like this, and thought about asking Hazel, but she might find it suspicious that I asked, so I decided to leave it. NDAs are part of my contract anyway, so at least we were both covered there.

It also made me wonder just how much money Hazel was spending on this endeavour, and where it all came from. Clearly she and Steven were very wealthy, but this seemed like obscene sums of money. This might be worth having a look into.

It was also time I looked a bit more into Steven, his death, and any family members who could be involved in this completely unproven stalking. It seemed like I'd been away from my office for so long that it felt really good to be back in there, churning away researching rather than hands-on investigating. The early signs of summer were starting to show, bringing the sun through my office window, illuminating my desk and bringing in a cheerful, warm, floral scent, which encouraged me to press on.

The internet is a fascinating place where you can find out most things about most people, so finding Steven Whittaker was not much of a challenge.

He had made his fortune in investments and property; I learned that Meadowview Cottage was owned outright, and the Whittakers also owned ten further properties in the area, which were rented out via an estate agent. This seemed to be where Hazel was getting her income from, on top of a very generous inheritance sum after Steven passed.

Steven had died in April the previous year of an aneurism. It was unexpected and sudden; he wasn't ill but one day he just dropped dead. I can't imagine the turmoil that must cause; to be there one minute and gone in the blink of an eye. Having experienced the long, drawn-out death of my father, I wondered which one is kinder on those involved. Before I could let my mind pull on that particular gloomy thread, I looked again at the date of Steven's death – 17 April. Hazel called me on 18 April; one year and one day after the sudden death of her husband. Could this be the trigger point of a breakdown causing all this paranoia? Could the real perpetrator of this be grief? Is all this suspicion the cause or the symptom? Before I went down that rabbit hole, I needed some more information.

I looked further into Steven's background, and hunted through news archives from the last ten years. I found that he had a son called Jamie, who was not Hazel's son. His mother and Steven had a brief relationship but parted ways before Jamie was born, but both parents shared equal responsibilities when it came to their son.

'What are you up to now, Jamie?' I asked myself as I blew the steam away from my mug of tea.

I immediately set my tea down before I could shoot it

across the room in shock. I let out an accidentally over-the-top 'oh my god' and cupped my face in disbelief. There it was, in black and white. I thought I'd worked it out and understood now why she thought someone was out to get her. They weren't; I was sure of it – more sure than I'd ever been. But now I needed to try to convince her.

'Were you planning on telling me about your late husband's son?' I asked her at our next meeting. By this point we were having face-to-face conversations once a week at different locations between her house and mine; I'd had little to tell her for some time now, but she insisted.

I watched the colour drain from her face and for a moment I thought I might have come at her a little harshly.

She wasn't looking at me, but staring down at her shiny black boots with a red sole. I couldn't help but think that, if I owned a pair of boots like that, I wouldn't wear them to a Starbucks at a service station on the M4. But then again, there were a lot of things about Hazel that I simply did not understand.

'Didn't you think your late husband's son's criminal conviction was relevant to you thinking you're being stalked, and that his upcoming release could have triggered your concerns?'

She didn't respond, but she looked like I'd slapped her in the face. This must have been the thing she felt she couldn't tell me. She seemed terrified. So I took a deep breath and changed my tone.

'I'm sorry this is difficult to talk about, and you must be finding this very painful.' I began to move my hand to delicately touch her shoulder, but then stopped myself; I didn't think that would help in this situation. 'I've also discovered that your husband died about a year before you reached out to me; a year before all this started . . .'

She looked up at me and I thought, she knows where I'm going with this so I need to tread very carefully.

'I've exhausted all avenues, searched the house multiple times, interviewed your neighbours, I've carried out surveillance on your house and there is absolutely no evidence to suggest that you're being watched or stalked, or that anyone is "out to get you", as you put it.'

I softly explained that I thought the anniversary of her husband's death, coupled with the situation with her stepson, Jamie, could have triggered a mental health episode.

For a brief moment she looked at me blankly, but that quickly turned to anger.

'You don't get it at all! That bastard son of his killed him and he is coming for me now! This is why I didn't tell you, I knew you'd think I'm making it all up!'

I was shocked by her outburst and confused that the story now changed to Jamie being the one out to get her, not her neighbours.

'I don't think you're making it all up, I think you

genuinely believe you are in danger, but what I'm trying to explain is that there's no evidence to suggest that and I think the help you need is not something I can give. Your husband died of an aneurysm, and Jamie was in jail at the time. There's no link.'

'I KNOW he did it and I know I'm next! That's why my neighbours want me out of my house, they're all working together to get me and when he gets out, he will – and it'll be your fault.'

Ah, that's the connection she'd made – everyone is in on it, apparently. She was bordering on hysterical and I tried to get her to calm down.

'They got to you!' She stood up, announcing it to the entire seating area. 'You're on their side, I knew I couldn't trust you!'

That stung. I'd done everything in my power to help her and she still couldn't see it.

'We're done here. Case closed.' She threw an envelope of cash at me and stormed out.

For a split second I thought about running after her, but I knew it would be pointless. So I just sat there, trying to process what had just happened and trying to ignore the stares of the other patrons. Hazel had made quite the scene, and everyone was looking, but thankfully no one was asking any questions.

A few moments later, Harvey came in to speak with me.

'Ms Whittaker no longer requires your service. She

said you should keep the money to cover any outstanding costs of your investigation but please do not contact her any more.' He looked genuinely apologetic, but I was still surprised by his following words. 'For what it's worth, I think you did a great job – she's not easy to work with and you stuck it out this far. Out of interest, could I see the notes?'

I refused, as it didn't seem right to hand over everything, but I gave him the top lines of my investigation and he just pursed his lips and nodded.

'Right-oh. All the best.' Then he left.

PI Perspective

I refer to Hazel's case often. Whenever I'm dealing with a particularly uncooperative client I think about Hazel and how difficult it was to chip away at her to understand her needs. The real villain of this story was the decline in her mental health. This, coupled with grief, made Hazel paranoid and combative; unable to accept the truth.

I felt a bit lost wrapping up this case as, despite my best efforts, I wasn't able to help Hazel. The help she needs is not something I, or any private investigator, could give her. I didn't really know what to make of how this investigation had ended – it certainly didn't go how I'd hoped, but I don't think I ever really expected it to.

After all, who can you trust if you can't even trust yourself?

CHAPTER 9

Taking Neighbourly Kindness Too Far

It's Always Closer Than You Think...

There have been cases where infidelity is hard to prove because it simply isn't there. And then there are cases where infidelity is hard to prove because it is in the only place you don't look – right under your nose.

George didn't think Cassie was cheating on him, but he noticed a lot of changes in her behaviour that gave him cause for concern. He told me he was only asking me to investigate her to eliminate cheating as a reason for her change. This was certainly an interesting take, and one that I hadn't heard before.

'I just want to completely confirm that she isn't cheating, so I can focus on what is really going on without the thought niggling in the back of my mind,' he explained when we met up after a few email exchanges.

They'd only been married for three years, after a two-year engagement, so in George's mind they were still very much in the honeymoon period of their relationship. They met when they were nineteen and, as many romcoms go, were friends for several years before they plucked up the courage to tell each other how they felt.

They didn't date for long – they already knew everything about each other from being such close friends – so they went straight into living together and then George got down on one knee just six months later.

'I don't know if you'd call it a whirlwind romance,' George explained, entirely unprompted – I didn't use the word whirlwind at all. 'More of, like, pieces falling into place at the right time. I think I always knew we'd be together, but I was far too scared of losing my best mate to do anything about it.'

George was one of the most charming men I had ever met – it was easy to see why someone would want to be his friend. He had kind eyes and a wide, bright smile. He was very animated and I keenly observed that he would talk with his hands a lot, which made his black-rimmed glasses slip down his face. Every few sentences he would push them up again, but they'd migrate down his thin nose within seconds.

It might sound odd, but this small quirk told me a lot about George. He was easy-going and had a lot of patience. You can tell a lot about people by their subtle idiosyncrasies and, if you can pick up on them, they can be really helpful in gauging a person's character.

George was constantly fidgeting, which told me that he wasn't sure he was making the right call, or that he was nervous to speak to me, so I questioned him on it.

'I'm a bit worried she will find out that I'm hiring a private investigator to spy on her – gosh it sounds mad when I say it out loud. I don't want her to think I don't trust her.'

I wince at the word spy; I'm not a spy and I don't look at what I do as spying on someone, but I understand the colloquialism, and it's much more quippy to say spying than 'conducting surveillance'. To me, spying sounds invasive and conjures an image of peeping through windows. I think surveillance is more stealthy; it's patiently watching from afar and to me it feels more ethical.

'Do you trust her, though?' I ask, because there must have been some level of mistrust there for him to get this far with me.

'I . . . I don't know for sure,' George replied, looking down. 'I think once you prove she isn't cheating, then I will.'

It doesn't quite work like that, I thought to myself. Once trust is broken, it doesn't just all fall back into place. Whatever the outcome of this investigation, it would change George and Cassie forever.

'This is a nice place,' George said, trying to change the subject. I found this very odd; he was acting like we were friends catching up, but I went with it to help him to feel more comfortable.

He was right, it was a really nice place. We met in Milton Keynes, which was a midway point between his home in Bedfordshire and mine in Oxfordshire. I chose a small, quiet cafe just off the main road for us to meet.

It was brightly lit, with signage on the walls displaying clichéd quotes like 'don't talk to me before my coffee' and 'there's never a wrong time for tea'. The walls were tiled in black with a few white and red ones dotted about, giving it a real American diner feel. Along the counter was a large display fridge filled with home-made cakes and pastries, which made me salivate every time I looked at them. George and I shared a few with several cups of tea while we talked.

'Yes, it was a good find. I think I'll come here again, perhaps next time we meet to discuss the case?' I said, trying to steer back to the topic at hand.

While I firmly believe intuition is a strong driver, I needed to know more about what led George to call me, so I asked him to explain the behaviour changes he had noticed in Cassie.

'Well, firstly it seemed like she was always on her phone, texting someone or just endlessly scrolling,' he began, picking at his half-eaten strawberry tart. 'I'm ashamed to admit that I tried to get onto her phone to see what she was doing, but she'd changed her passcode. It was always the same four digits and we've always sort of shared phones – I'd use hers, she'd use mine – so I couldn't fathom why she changed it. I don't understand why she locked me out?'

He went on to explain that the passcode had changed for her tablet, and she'd removed WhatsApp from her laptop. 'That really got me thinking that she was hiding something,' he explained, again pushing his glasses up his nose.

There were other signs too, he went on. Cassie had completely changed the way she dressed, she had started curling her hair when it was always straight, she was a lot busier than she used to be, couldn't attend family functions, among others.

'I just miss her, you know? I miss us. We used to be so in sync and connected, now we feel distant. There's a wall between us and I want to find out what it is. If it's someone else . . .' He paused and then laughed at the idea. 'No, it can't be, it just . . . it just can't.' He let out a long sigh through his nose and picked at the strawberry tart some more with one hand, adjusting his glasses (again) with the other.

'Well, let's hope my investigation can help you figure it out,' I said sympathetically.

The signs were there, but they could easily be dismissed as something else. I needed to find some evidence. I hoped for his peace of mind I found *something*, but I really hoped it wasn't that Cassie was cheating.

George was quite specific about what he wanted me to investigate – I love it when clients have specifics in mind; it makes the whole process much smoother and saves me a lot of time (and them a lot of money).

He wanted to know if there were any cars in their driveway during the day and if anyone went in or out of the house; if so, he wanted to know if she left and for how long. He didn't want me to follow her, just observe the home.

George worked as a photographer at a studio approximately thirty minutes away and Cassie worked from home creating fitness videos on YouTube. According to my research, she was quite popular and as such they had built a studio at the end of their garden for her to work from. He told me she rarely left the house during the day, except to nip to the shops or go for a run, and that recording and editing her content was a 9–5 for her.

After signing contracts, I got to work and set off for a day (or more) of surveillance from outside the house.

The drive from my house to George and Cassie's was only about an hour – traffic depending. I set off at about 10am and would stay outside the house until George got home at between 5:30 and 6pm. It was quite a short stake-out compared to what I'm used to, but I would be doing this every day for a week, so over time it would build up to quite a lot of hours outside the same house.

They lived on quite a busy street, lined with terraced houses. Most homes had wide driveways, big enough for two cars, but some had picturesque front gardens. George and Cassie's home (with a driveway) had a yellow brick facade and a solid wood black front door with the number

17 and floral details etched into the glass at the top. The door was on the right, with the driveway on the left, and thick shrubbery surrounding it in lieu of a fence or gate. Next to the door was a row of sunflowers, beautifully blooming in the summer sun.

I parked up a few houses down with a good view of the house and any incoming traffic. It was quite a busy street with a lot of foot traffic, so I felt a bit exposed. It was a sunny day, and the sunshine was hitting my windscreen, which I hoped would obscure me enough to sit here unnoticed for several hours.

As it often is with surveillance, I waited and waited and nothing happened. No one visited the house and Cassie didn't leave. So when George arrived back a little after 5:30, I left with nothing to show for the day.

The following day was a little more interesting as, when I arrived at about 11am, there was a new car in the driveway. I drove past the house several times to see if I could catch any of its details, but it was parked so tightly I couldn't see the registration, nor the make and model. All I knew was that it was long and silver – nothing remarkable at all.

I sighed to myself and craned my neck to look up at the sky. It was typical that it would be today – when it was chucking it down with rain – that I needed to get out of the car.

Rule number one of private investigation: always be prepared!

I reached over to the passenger seat for my trusty PI kit and grabbed a black baseball cap and my pull-over raincoat. It was thin and flowery and added no warmth at all, but at least it should keep my top half from getting drenched. I secured the hat and took a quick look in the mirror in my sun visor. 'It's acting time,' I said to myself, then chuckled at the silliness.

I'd chosen to park a little further away because I would approach on foot and it would look odd if I got out of the car right near the house.

This was great for anonymity but really not ideal for my feet, which wore canvas plimsolls – should have put boots on, I chastised myself as I stepped in a puddle. I reached into the pocket of my practically useless raincoat and pulled out a small, pink, sparkly cat collar with a loud bell.

'Luna? Luuunaaa?' I called as I got near to number 17. Some pedestrians were approaching, so I wanted to show I had a reason to be there (other than because I was conducting an investigation on a resident, obviously).

'Excuse me, sorry, have you seen my cat? She's all black but has a blob of white on her face and white paws.'

They mumbled no sorry and kept walking, and I kept calling the name of the non-existent cat as I approached number 17.

'Luna? Is that you?' I said as I reached the house, and peered over the bush, snapping a sneaky photograph of the rear of the mystery car.

TAKING NEIGHBOURLY KINDNESS TOO FAR

'Come on Luna, where are you?' I carried on my ruse as I passed the house, then, when I was safely out of view, I walked round the block and back to my car.

As is typical with British weather (and my luck with it), the rain stopped as soon as I reached my car. I opened the boot and kicked off my now dripping wet plimsolls and put on a fresh pair of socks and my boots. My black leggings were uncomfortably damp, so I wriggled out of them as soon as I got into the car. Thankfully the flimsy raincoat had gone some way to keeping my dress dry, so at least I didn't have to change it and risk flashing the street.

Feeling pumped that I'd made a bit of progress, I sent a text to George asking if it was a good time to talk. I then drove round closer to number 17 to keep observing the house while I waited for his reply.

It was a long two hours waiting to hear back from George, and during that time the car left, but I didn't manage to capture the person getting into it as the rain started again and they were obscured by a large umbrella – I don't know why someone would need an umbrella for five steps, and I found it really frustrating.

I still hadn't actually seen Cassie, but I had subscribed to her YouTube channel (under an assumed identity) and had received a notification to say she had recently uploaded. I watched the video, and I could tell by the rain beating down on the windows of her studio that it was filmed this morning, so she was definitely home.

Who could the mystery visitor be if Cassie was filming

content? This realisation took the edge off the suspicion, but then again I didn't know how long it took to film and edit a workout video.

When George finally did respond, I texted him the image I'd snapped of the car and asked if he recognised it. George was quite passionate about this investigation, so I wasn't shocked when he called me a few seconds after the 'read' receipt popped up.

'Ali, I'm so sorry, I made a mistake,' he announced hurriedly. I took a sharp inhale and braced myself for what was to come next. Was he tapping out already? Was this the proof he needed?

'I forgot to tell you our cleaner was coming today, and their car would be in the driveway,' he explained, and my entire body released the tension I didn't realise it was holding.

I slumped down in my seat and let out a sigh – part relief, part frustration. I rubbed my face and then pinched the bridge of my nose. 'Ok . . . that makes sense as Cassie was clearly working this morning. Any other visitors I should be aware of?'

'Nope, none.'

We ended the call and I put my head in my hands with disappointment.

Day three came and went with absolutely nothing and I was starting to get antsy. I'd clocked about eighteen hours of watching number 17 with little to show for it and I was starting to wonder if a change of approach was needed.

Day four, however, had me jumping out of my skin, and put my skill in talking myself out of things to the test.

I tried to park in different places each day, and every few hours I would do a lap around the nearby streets to make sure it wasn't obvious that I was waiting there in my car. I tried everything I could to mask myself; pretended to read a book, pretended to be on the phone and so on, but on day four I was clocked.

The tapping on my window startled me, causing me to launch my phone into the air. It landed somewhere under my seat. I opened the window just enough to hear the raised voice of a person outside.

It was a tall man with olive skin and an impressive moustache. He was dressed in joggers, a vest and (as I learned when he walked away) a pair of Crocs – with socks.

'Are you watching me?' he asked. My eyes widened and I tried to calm the rising panic in my chest.

'Pardon?' I said, trying to buy some time.

'I've seen this car here loads, every day this week, with you sitting in it. Are you watching me?'

'I'm really not sure what you mean,' I said, calming the wobble in my voice.

'Are. You. Watching. Me?!' he said slowly and determinedly, the anger in his voice increasing with every word.

'No sir, not at all. I've only been here today,' I said cheerfully. 'I'm just waiting to check up on a friend. She's been unwell but hasn't answered her phone today, so I thought I'd pop by and see if she's okay, but she texted me just before you knocked, and I was just about to leave. I'd show you but my phone is somewhere under my seat as you startled me.' I shot him a wide smile and my kindest eyes, hoping he'd buy it.

'Hmm,' he said and walked off.

Shit. Shit shit shit, I said to myself as I started the car and pulled away. I called George immediately and told him I would have to suspend surveillance for a few days until the heat died down. It wasn't worth risking the investigation or my safety to come back tomorrow.

I picked off every single sliver of nail varnish on my fingers as I drove home. I'd never been noticed before, so it was startling and I felt really flapped by it. I knew it was a bit risky being on that street for so many days in a row, but I didn't expect Joe Nobody to notice me, let alone ask me about it.

I went home, poured a large gin and flopped in front of the TV for a while – a new plan would come to me, but not now, now I needed to relax.

Are you watching me?

Are you watching me?

Are

You

Watching me?

The words went round and round my mind all night. I

barely slept a wink. Not only was it frightening, but it had brought up a lot of feelings about what I do.

I knew in my heart that my only goal was to help my clients and help them find a resolution – but I'd never stopped to think about the people caught in the crosshairs before.

I liked to think I was morally sound and as ethical as I could be – but could a PI really *be* completely ethical? I didn't think I knew the answer, and the question kept me awake all night.

The following morning, I looked in the mirror as I brushed my teeth – the bad night's sleep was written all over my face. I really needed a day to collect myself and reposition this case.

After a much-needed bucket of tea and some plain toast – all my stomach could handle – I gave George a call, hoping to catch him before he started work.

He answered quickly and I could hear the sound of the road in the background, so I assumed he was still on his commute.

'Hi George, I just wanted to reach out about the incident yesterday.'

'Yes, I bet that was a shock for you – are you okay? Based on your description, I think that was Scott. He and his wife live next door and they're very nosey,' George explained, and I appreciated him asking after me.

It didn't feel appropriate to tell him how it had rattled me, so I brushed it off with, 'Oh, it's just part of the job.'

'Well, that's good. I assume you won't be along today just in case?'

'That's right, I hope you understand.'

'Yes, of course. But I did a bit of digging myself.' This brought my whole body to attention, as it often complicates the investigation when a client tries to pitch in. I waited on edge for him to continue.

'We have a WhatsApp chat of some of the residents down the street, we started it during the pandemic so we could help each other out, so I asked if anyone could take in a parcel for me and Scott replied saying he can do any day but Monday as that's when he works in the office. So I think it'll be safe if you come back then.'

Relieved that he hadn't gone too far, I thanked him for this information. I already felt a bit better knowing that the chances of getting spotted again were much slimmer with Scott out of the picture, but I still felt unsure of myself.

I was sitting in my office with my head in my hands and my feet lightly perched on Barry's belly under my desk. He was very good at telling when I was rattled, so he stuck by me the whole day. Every time my feet would get twitchy, as they often did when I was stressed, he would gently hold them in his paw, or give a very delicate nibble if he sensed I was particularly antsy.

I needed to talk with someone in the same position – I wanted to know how other PIs reacted when they were noticed during an investigation – so I turned to the UKPIN, which is an unmatched source of support and information.

I learned that it is very common for this to happen – the fact that I was several years in and it hadn't happened yet was actually a sign of a good investigator; it made me feel a bit more confident knowing this. As I read through other experiences, I felt the cloud lift a little. There had been incidents where investigators had been caught and fights started, and I was thankful that my altercation was very minor – a perspective that I greatly needed.

I turned my head up to the right, and my eyes were drawn to a poster my daughter Alexis made for me right at the start of my career that I had completely forgotten about. It read:

ALWAYS REMEMBER THE 3 Ms
MOTIVE
METHOD
MISS AM

This was a mantra I had thought up years ago to keep me grounded, and I was a bit disappointed in myself for letting my discomfort get in the way of remembering it. The series of words had a set of questions tied to them, and their answers would determine whether I was doing the right thing.

Motive: Why did the client need this information?

Was it for nefarious reasons? Was I clear about what they would do with the information?

Method: Is everything legal? Could any acts be seen as entrapment? Am I forcing the narrative by putting the pieces together in an inaccurate way or missing out certain aspects?

Miss AM: Am I being true to who Miss AM is? Am I compromising my integrity? Have I given false hope? Am I so driven to find answers that I miss the bigger picture?

I went through the questions on a notepad, jotting down my answers and corresponding thoughts. I sat back in my chair, held my notepad in both hands and scrutinised every word I had written.

I tapped my fingers on the back of the notepad, nodded, and realised I was doing my best by my client and operating in the right ways. I pushed my doubts out of my mind and went about my day, ready to get back to the case on Monday.

My stomach was a ball of nerves again by Monday morning when I prepared to set off for George and Cassie's house for my fifth and final day of surveillance. I wasn't convinced that I would find anything; so far there had been so little activity that I didn't hold out much hope. Without physically seeing Cassie, I couldn't tell anything about her.

George had assured me that Scott shouldn't be home and that it would be safe for me to conduct surveillance without being noticed, but to be safe I borrowed Mark's car as an extra layer of security.

I hate driving Mark's car – it's much bulkier than mine and makes an infuriating clunking sound whenever it changes gears. I grabbed my PI kit from my boot and chucked it in the footwell of Mark's before setting off. I got to the end of the road and the fuel light came on, and I cursed Mark for always driving on near-empty.

I pulled into the nearest garage and grabbed a hot drink along with the fuel. Before setting off – again – I quickly texted Mark to inform him of his oversight using several expletives.

It was raining again, so the roads were quite busy. This combined with the unexpected fuel stop meant that I arrived later than usual, at about 11:30. All day I sat and watched, but nothing happened until 2:30, when I finally saw Cassie in the flesh.

She was much taller than she appeared in pictures and in her videos. She had a classically beautiful face with soft features and pink cheeks. Her hair was tied up in a hairband so impossibly high that the curled ends bobbed and swung from side to side with every step.

She had keys and her purse in her hand, and moved with intention. I started the car, ready to follow wherever she went. She crossed the road and went down an alleyway so I couldn't follow in my car. I didn't know where it led, so I pulled over near the entrance. I could see Cassie moving through it. At the other side there appeared to be a butcher's and a small convenience store. She hopped into the latter and came out again a few minutes later with a carrier bag.

I reversed my car as soon as she entered the alleyway. She was looking at her phone, so hopefully she didn't see me. She went straight back into the house and I didn't see her again.

I honestly thought about calling it a day and telling George that I thought we should either try something else, or wrap up entirely. But something in me told me to stick around.

As 5:45 rolled round and George's car returned to the driveway, I wished I had listened to myself earlier. I let out a long sigh and said, 'Well, that's that' to myself as I started the engine. As I left the street, I saw a car pull up in front of the house next door which stopped me in my tracks, I then saw Scott get out and head into his house. I hadn't realised I'd been holding my breath, so as soon as the door closed, I gasped for air. Shaking my head, I put the car into gear and started off home.

In five days I only saw Cassie once, and all she did was go to the shop. There were no visitors other than the cleaner, and from her social media and YouTube activity she appeared to be working all day long. George told me they spent the whole weekend together, and that everything seemed normal then. There was nothing to suggest anything untoward was going on, and I thought we could chalk this up to just a blip in their relationship.

TAKING NEIGHBOURLY KINDNESS TOO FAR

As I hit the main road back to Oxfordshire, I got a call from George. I answered it using the Bluetooth in my car.

'She's going for a run!' he declared in what could only be described as a loud whisper. 'She never goes at this time and she's just had a shower – can you get back and see where she's going? You've got about ten minutes. She's wearing make-up – she never runs in make-up!'

There was noticeable panic in his voice, which put my whole body on edge. I inadvertently mirrored his panic and frantically responded, 'Ok, okay, I'll be there.' Something about his tone sent shockwaves through my body. The tiredness and disappointment I had felt only moments ago was brushed away as my senses ignited at the possibility of cracking the case. It was thrilling!

I checked my rear-view mirror, carefully hit the brakes and signalled to turn off the road back to number 17.

'I've turned round, I'm on my way,' I declared. I cut the call off so I wasn't distracted and drove as fast and safely and the law would permit me to get back in time.

As I drove past number 17 I could see George at the window – he'd pulled back the curtains and was looking left and right down the road to watch for me coming. I caught his eyes, and saw a look of relief wash over him.

The rain had stopped, so it was plausible that Cassie would have gone out now. Perhaps it was too wet this morning. I felt like she deserved the benefit of the doubt now.

I parked across the road just one house over. I had a view of the alleyway and number 17 from here.

I saw the front door open, and Cassie left the house. Her hair was down, with the curls framing her round face – she looked like a model, which I thought was odd for a run. She flicked her hair over her shoulder as she put on her headphones and walked down the driveway to the street.

She was dressed in athletic gear – black shorts with a white trim, a tight-fitting pale pink vest and trainers that looked expensive, gleaming white in a stark contrast with the puddled street. Her phone was in a holster on her right arm.

She stood there stretching for a few minutes, looking back at the house with every lunge. George was gone from the window now, and after a final look at the house she began to jog.

I kept an eye on her as she pounded the pavement with her bright trainers, and was confused when she came to a stop after only a few yards. She looked back again, craning her neck round the bush. Then she began walking, checking behind with every other step, and pushed open the gate to the house next door.

With my phone in hand, I wound down the window to remove the left-over raindrops from the earlier shower and took a few photos.

Cassie reached into her pocket (how those tiny shorts had pockets is beyond me) and pulled out something small, which I quickly learned was a key. As she put it into the lock, the door was opened by the mystery occupier, who immediately grabbed her and pulled her into an embrace, kissing her passionately.

It was Scott.

The busybody neighbour who challenged me a few days ago for watching him. No wonder he was concerned; George had told me he had a wife.

I didn't have time to react. I had to capture the footage before he closed the door. I managed to snap several shots of them kissing before the door closed.

'What the . . .' I said to myself, zooming in on the photos to make sure I saw correctly.

When I was sure the coast was clear, I got out of the car and went and knocked on George's door. This couldn't wait.

He answered quickly, and was agog to see me standing there, not Cassie. He quickly ushered me inside, checking behind me.

The house was beautifully decorated with mint-green flowery wallpaper. The small entryway led into a huge open-plan kitchen with deep mahogany cupboards and a range cooker I was very envious of.

George clicked the kettle on, then off again immediately. 'Sorry, I would make tea but I don't know how long we have and how to explain you to Cass when she's back from her run.'

He was so bubbly and optimistic, a far cry from the

shaky, nervous man I had spoken to on the phone not long ago.

'So I take it you saw her go for a run, all is good?' he asked brightly.

Oof, this was not going to be a nice conversation. I just had to rip the plaster off and get it over with.

'George, I'm so sorry, but no. All is not good. She's next door. I saw her kissing Scott and she went inside.'

'What?' he said, as if this information was completely out of the blue and he'd forgotten that he'd asked me to find it. 'Can't have been Cass . . .' He paused for a moment and put his hands together in front of his face as if he was praying it away. 'Are you sure?'

I turned my phone screen to him to show him the evidence. 'I'm certain,' I said with authority.

'Can you please send me that?' he asked me calmly. He was suddenly so still and collected compared to the lively George I'd seen before that I found it unnerving. I quickly sent the images over without looking at him.

'Do you want to talk it over?' I asked, quite sure of the answer already.

'No . . . thank you, I think maybe you should go,' he said, moving towards the front door.

'Of course. I'm very sorry this didn't end how you wanted it to. I will be in touch in a few days to hand over everything and close this up.'

'Ok, thank you,' he said without meeting my eyes, and slowly shut the door behind me.

I wanted to be anywhere but here right now, so I quickly jumped in the car and began to drive off. As I turned the corner I saw George in my rear-view mirror, heading to the house next door.

George didn't respond to me after this day, so I don't know what the conclusion was. But from a quick social media check a few weeks later, it seemed he and Cassie were separated. Her YouTube channel carried on from the same location, but beyond that I had no details. George simply paid the bill when I emailed it over along with all the documentation from the case and that was it. Case closed on George and Cassie.

PI Perspective

While there is no definitive 'who' women cheat with, statistically women have affairs with people they already know. It's not often a spur of the moment flash of weakness, typically it's more planned. In my experience, a woman decides if and when she will cheat and with whom, whereas cheating seems to just 'happen' with a man. Studies show that cheating men are usually motivated by sexual desire, whereas women cheat to fill an emotional need. Lack of intimacy within the relationship, low self-esteem, anger or retribution or even loneliness can all be the catalyst that makes the woman decide to cheat.

The reason for Cassie's cheating is unknown. I don't know how long it had been going on for (long enough for her to have a key to his house...) or why it started – and sadly I'll never know.

I like to keep in touch with my clients – I think we create a strong bond during the process and often I'm the only person who they can talk to about the case – so I found it disappointing when George made it clear he didn't want any further contact. Of course I respected his decision, but there were still questions looming. Often, I get a chance to discuss the resolution and help my client navigate through the new normal, but that wouldn't be the case here.

The hardest part of this case was how it shook my sense of security and made me question my ethics. Scott's demeanour had left me feeling on edge after our run-in on the street the week prior, but it made a lot more sense why he was so rattled at the thought of my watching him, as he was also cheating. According to George, Scott had a wife, so he was equally guilty in this mess. Knowing this made it easier to accept that I hadn't intentionally done anything to hurt Scott, and he was caught in the crosshairs of his own doing.

I just pray I don't get clocked again!

CHAPTER 10

Dognapping

A Not-Really-A-Case Case

Every investigation is emotionally draining; it's complicated and exhausting spending every day learning the new ways that people are treated terribly. Some days it can be really difficult to put on my investigator hat (metaphorically; as we've covered, I don't wear a bloody hat) and get on with it. That's even more difficult when something I care about is at the heart of the case.

In March 2020, the UK went into its first national lockdown to prevent the spread of Covid-19. In fact, most of the world locked down in one way or another, so chances are it impacted your life in some way. While I'm not here to argue the effectiveness of the UK government during this time (though I have my thoughts, as I'm sure you do too), we can unanimously agree there was a huge loss. Whether it was the loss of life, the loss of jobs, the loss of companionship, the difficulty was felt across the nation.

A rather unexpected loss during this time came from a spate of dog thefts that swept across the nation during lockdown. According to data from Direct Line Insurance, there was a 31 per cent rise in dog thefts in 2020, and (though numbers vary) over the last five years this has increased again, with an average of seven dogs now being stolen every day.

This problem struck a nearby village and was brought to my attention by a local Neighbourhood Watch group. They'd posted on their website that they wanted to discuss this crime wave, and I knew as a proud pooch-parent to my own pup, I needed to be involved on a professional and a personal level.

The level of concern was so high, a face-to-face meeting was arranged for the residents to get together to discuss it. It had been a few months since the pandemic was declared, and social distancing was fully enforced.

Because of this, the local town hall filled up quickly; for every four seats, there would be only one person. These meetings only happen once or twice a year and cover several districts in the area, so they're often quite full. When crime hits a small area like this, lots of people have a stake in it, and I knew it would be a stronger than usual turnout. Coupled with the loneliness that isolation and stay-at-home orders bring, the room was as heaving as it legally could be.

DOGNAPPING

Thankfully I managed to get in, and was able to hear the stories of dog thefts from people who lived in the local area.

Standing at a lectern on the small community hall stage that was usually home to the local school's plays and the choir's biannual concert were the chairpersons of the Neighbourhood Watch committee – a very lively, friendly elderly chap named Terrence (never Terry), and a young, sprightly resident named Billy (never Bill).

The hall smelt exactly like any other hall – dusty and cold, with a faint whiff of old PE kit. The heavy dark-green stage curtains hung lifelessly to the sides and in front of them were about ten rows of chairs, each with only ten chairs instead of the usual twenty plus. There were also about twenty-five people standing at the back and along the sides, all obeying the strict distancing laws. It was strange – it felt like we were all too early for something, or perhaps the stragglers at the end of one of the rare disco nights held here.

They addressed the crowd, explaining that this wave of crime was nationwide but had affected several local residents, and invited them to get up and share their stories.

The waves of concern that rippled through the small crowd were palpable. I had a notebook and pen in hand and listened to each story on the edge of my seat.

First to speak was a dear friend of mine, Susan, who lives just one road over from me. She timidly approached the middle of the stage with a crumpled piece of lined paper in her shaking hand. Susan hates crowds, so it took a lot of courage for her to get up there. We hadn't spoken for a week, so this is the first I'd heard that she was a victim. Susan's garden backs on to mine and occasionally one (or both) of our dogs would dig under the fence to bounce between the gardens and play together. I felt a huge stab of guilt for not noticing sooner, and sick to my stomach that this crime was so close to home.

'Thank you everyone for being here today. I know it's a bit scary being in a crowd with everything that's going on, so I really appreciate everyone caring about this.' Susan looked up and caught my eye, I gave her a sympathetic smile as a tear rolled down her cheek.

'A few days ago, I tied my dog up outside the corner shop like I do almost every day. I popped in and grabbed a few items – it couldn't have been more than five minutes – and when I came out, Frilly was gone.' Hushed tones and gasps moved their way through the room.

Frilly was a pure-breed Yorkshire terrier. She was a beautiful little thing with long fur that was a mix of tan and grey, with a petite face and a nose that looked like a leather button. I couldn't help but think that, if you were going to steal a dog, Frilly would be the prime target.

Next to speak was Mr Pritchett, who ran the allotments about ten miles away. His cocker spaniel, Bear, was a working dog, who assisted in keeping the allotments vermin-free.

'He was a soppy thing with long droopy ears, but he

was a champion rat-chaser. He was so fast and so strong, I'm beside myself thinking about how someone could have got hold of him. He's well trained and comes on command but he isn't returning no matter how loud I shout, so he must be far away and unable to escape.'

We then heard stories from another three victims – one successful theft, one attempted, and one taken but then found.

'I'd been told if you advertise a reward for a missing dog and create a lot of buzz about it, there's a chance that thieves will . . . you know . . . destroy the evidence . . .' This speaker was Gillian, the only victim to actually recover their missing pet. She also had a cocker spaniel, Rosie, who she used to breed, but as they both got older she stopped and had Rosie spayed.

The shudders that echoed through the hall when she said 'destroy the evidence' almost rattled the windows. Everyone knew what she meant – there was a possibility that the stolen dog would be killed.

'Then I got a phone call from an unknown number and they said they had Rosie and would return her to me and collect the reward. They said they spotted her on the side of the main road and took her to the vets, where they spotted my poster, so they called me instead. I was so happy to have her home that I didn't ask for details. I wish I had now because I don't believe she was just found. I think the people who took her returned her for the money when they realised they couldn't breed her. The reward was worth more than what she could do for them.'

I noted this down and underlined it three times. I could feel that pulling sensation in my gut that told me I needed to dig deeper. There was something going on here and I needed to find out what and why.

The two almost-thefts were very similar in circumstance and the same as Susan's story. The dogs were tied up outside and left unattended for a few minutes, and were gone by the time the owner came back – however on both occasions, the dogs were close by and ran back when called. There was too much activity and coincidence for these to be crimes of chance. They seemed methodical and thought-out. This was being orchestrated by a person or a group of people and I think we all knew it.

I decided there and then that I needed to investigate this. This investigation would be different on many levels; primarily because I didn't have a client. I was doing this pro bono because it was the right thing to do.

I sat on the uncomfortable plastic chair trying to think – I had to quickly decide whether I should announce that I was investigating and encourage people to talk to me, or keep it to myself. It would be easier to talk to the right people if they came to me, but equally it could alert the thieves to my investigation and make it harder.

'Is there anyone else who'd like to speak?' Billy asked the hall. There were some mumblings but no one raised their hands. I had about ten seconds to make a decision.

My entire body was a bundle of nerves. My foot was twitching, my eyes darting around the room, my inner lip raw from me chewing on it. I didn't know what to do.

'Ok, well, that wraps it up for this evening,' Billy announced. okay, decision made, I said to myself. 'Thank you for coming and for obeying social distancing rules. Stay safe.'

The already thin crowd thinned out some more but I made sure to position myself by the exit to catch the speakers before they left.

Susan came over looking half sad but half inquisitive. We'd been neighbours for years and I thought she'd know me well enough to know what I was thinking.

'Let me guess . . . you'd like to set up a time for us to have a chat about what's going on?' she asked jokingly.

'That is exactly what I'd like!' We made a plan for me to go to her house the following day to get as much detail as I could.

'I'm not paying you though!' she said as she left, and we both let out a huge cathartic laugh.

I knew Susan would want me to help, but I wasn't sure if the others would think I was gossiping or prying. I didn't think anyone else knew what my job was, so I'd have to approach this very carefully.

Mr Pritchett was talking to Gillian, so I could hopefully convince them both at the same time. I confidently approached them, planning my opener as I crossed the creaky hall.

'Excuse me, I wondered if you had some time to speak more in depth about your experience. I live in the village and I'm a private investigator and dog owner, so I want to be able to help where I can. Any information you give me could really help.'

They both looked very surprised to be approached. Given their recent traumas, it was reasonable for them to have their guards up and be suspicious of any stranger. But once I explained that my intentions were purely to try to stop this from happening and, if I was very lucky, be able to return some lost loved ones, they agreed to speak with me.

By the time I left the hall, I had a meeting booked with every victim – not bad for a night's work.

My first objective was to get as much information out of the victims as I could, and then piece together each story, generate a timeline, and then compare to see if there were any overlapping dates or circumstances. A lot of the stories sounded similar, but I needed to pick out some more details to really understand.

At this point I was back home and having a quiet moment in my garden. The summer sun was beginning to set, showering my garden in a beautiful dusky glow, casting long shadows against the shrubbery. It was so peaceful and serene that you wouldn't have thought the world was at war with a virus.

A light flicking on caught my eye and I looked to

the end of the garden and up at Susan's house; a stark reminder of the criminal epidemic that had hit our quaint village. Why was this happening? I had to find out, and I would.

Barry was, of course, at my feet, and, despite knowing my lap would suffer, I gave my thighs an intentional pat to encourage him to leap up onto me. I couldn't bear the thought of something happening to this old fool.

That got me thinking about my dad – as I often did sitting in this chair, but more so since the stay-at-home orders came in. I wondered how different things would be if he was still around. I know for a fact I'd have packed a suitcase or two and gone to stay with him – I couldn't have left him alone in all this. Alexis lived with her partner and I was sure Mark would be okay; I'd probably have left Barry here, which just made me feel sick all over again.

I took another glance across the garden, almost entirely in shadow now as the sun had almost set. I gulped the dregs of my cup of tea and sighed a heavy, cathartic sigh. Nothing I could do tonight, so I stood up (much to Barry's disgust) and headed off to bed. I didn't expect to sleep well, but as soon as I hit the pillow I was gone.

I spent the following morning in a state of melancholy. Any enthusiasm I had for the case melted away and I was left feeling a bit stuck. I dressed and looked in the mirror, ready to have a talk with myself, but I struggled to recognise the woman looking back at me. It was like I was in sepia tones; my classic red hair was fading and with it had gone some of the light in my eyes. I'd read about how the pandemic was causing a lot of people to feel isolated, leading to depression, and wondered if that feeling was creeping in here. I've always been quite in tune with my mental wellbeing, having struggled for many years, so I took some time to remind myself to look after myself, especially during this case, which was bound to stir up a lot of emotions.

Having shaken off some of the gloom, I took the short walk round to Susan's house. I didn't plan on going in, I thought we could just stand by her door to talk as I didn't want to break any social distancing rules. Susan clearly had the same idea, as when I approached her gate I could see her setting up a small table and chairs on the front lawn.

Susan was very green-fingered, with well-tended plants and trees in her gardens. I opened the slightly creaky iron gate and walked through under the breathtaking canopy of a magnolia tree, which momentarily transported me to paradise as I breathed in the sweet scent of the flowers. On the gate swung a small plaque saying:

BEWARE OF THE DOG – HE MIGHT LICK YOU TO DEATH

. . . which for a brief moment made me smile, then I remembered why I was here and a wave of sadness washed over me.

Susan looked surprisingly upbeat, considering what she was going through. She lived alone, having lost her husband some years ago to heart disease, and her four children had moved away. Her house was the same size as mine (fairly spacious but nothing too grand) but she had a double extension at the back and had built up into the loft to accommodate her big family. Now they were all gone I worried about her rattling about in this big house all alone. She had Frilly and I knew she brought Susan a great sense of companionship, but now she was gone and my heart broke for her.

We sat down on the wrought-iron seats and both slowly dipped lower as the feet of the chairs sank into the grass. It made us both let out a laugh we really needed. The air felt clearer, and we got to work.

Susan recounted the story she'd shared the previous night at the town hall, and I ferociously made notes. Unfortunately, beyond the matter-of-fact details, Susan couldn't recall many others, despite my many probing questions.

Did you see anything out of the ordinary? Can't recall.

Did you hear any commotion while in the shop? Can't recall.

Did Frilly bark? Can't recall.

This was completely understandable (albeit frustrating) as, when you go about your everyday business like you do all the time, it can be easy to switch into autopilot and not pay much attention to anything else.

I left Susan's with not much more information than I had already, except I knew the exact day and time the theft took place, which I could insert into the timeline I'd been creating.

Over the following days I met with all the victims of the crimes, and no one else had much more information.

I created a timeline on the corkboard in my office, and stuck up pictures of each missing pet chronologically, adding the key details each witness shared with me. I used pins and different-coloured strips of ribbon to make connections between timings and quotes. Mark lovingly mocked me for this, asking if I'd started a job with the CIA that I'd forgotten to tell him about.

My phone buzzed on my desk, rattling everything on it and startling me. It was a number I didn't recognise.

'Hello, this is Miss AM Investigations, how can I help?'

'Is that Ali? Gillian gave me your number, she said you're looking into the missing dogs.'

'Yes, I am. Do you have information?'

'You could say that . . . I've just been mugged and they tried to take my dog.'

Alarm bells started ringing in my head, along with a thousand questions.

'Are you okay? I think you should call the police.'

'I have, they took a report but didn't care about the dog part. Didn't even write it down. As nothing was actually stolen they said there's nothing they can do.'

'Where are you? Can I come and meet you now?'

'I'm in the park, near the playground.'

DOGNAPPING

The park was a short drive from my house, so it wouldn't take me long to meet her.

'I'll be there soon.'

We hung up and I realised I hadn't even asked for her name, but I felt like she needed someone with her, and it would be the best time for me to take the details I would need.

I hotfooted it to the park and found a young woman, early twenties I guessed, sitting on a bench holding on to her dog tightly. She looked frightened, with tears streaming down her face.

I sat down next to her and introduced myself, and learned her name was Zola, and her dog was called Chestnut – Chessie for short.

Don't tell Barry, but this dog was the most beautiful dog I'd ever seen. She was a chocolate-brown cockapoo with a coat so shiny the summer sun made her almost glisten. She had tight, perfectly formed ringlets all over her back and smooth waves of fur on her sides and legs. Her ears were long with the same waves as her body, and she had a tuft of curls on her head that looked like she had a quiff.

Seeing her immediately triggered a connection in my mind – another beautiful, popular breed of dog targeted. I put a mental pin in it so I could focus all of my attention on Zola.

She was still shaking, so I helped her steady herself by encouraging her to take long, slow breaths. With every rise and fall of her chest I could sense the terror leaving her body.

I asked her if she felt ready to tell me what happened and she took a deep, intentional breath and let out a long sigh of relief.

'I have walked Chessie in this park every single day for a year and nothing like this has ever happened,' she began. There were those words again; she was following her usual daily routine.

'Over the fields she was off the lead but a few minutes before it happened I had clipped her back in as we were getting near the playground. She's very friendly but I think it's safer for everyone if she's on a lead near the kids.'

I love a responsible dog owner, I thought to myself.

'I'm usually quite alert and aware of my surroundings, so when I noticed the area was quite empty apart from a group of about five men my guard went up, and I pulled Chessie closer. Something felt off, so I actually turned to walk in the other direction, but that didn't seem to stop them, and they started after me.'

She let out a sob and I took her hand and reassured her that she was safe now.

'It then happened so fast; they clustered around me so I couldn't go anywhere and one grabbed the lead. I had a tight grip and it really hurt my hand, but I wasn't going to let go. They threatened to hurt me if I didn't hand her over.'

I looked down at her hand in mine and could see redness and grazing from where they had tugged at the lead.

'I don't know why the thought popped into my head but I shouted, "She's spayed, she's spayed!" I told them she was worthless and they couldn't breed her.' She gave Chessie an extra-tight cuddle and a kiss on her curly head as if to say, 'I didn't mean it, you're not worthless'.

'With that, they just looked at each other and grumbled, then they ran away.'

Zola's story confirmed in my head what I'd suspected from the moment I found out about this crime wave. I believed there was a group of people stealing popular dog breeds and pedigrees in order to breed them for profit. I wanted to investigate why this was happening and see if there was anything I could do to stop it, but this was turning out to be much bigger than I'd expected. If there was unethical dog breeding happening in the village, hopefully I could gather some evidence to share with the police and bring some reassurance to my neighbours.

A puppy farm or mill is where multiple dogs are continuously bred and the puppies sold for gargantuan profit. Typically, breeders of this ilk do not care about animal welfare and will use the dogs over and over again without veterinary care or the love and attention they deserve. Vaccinations and other usual aspects of breeding are overlooked in order to make a quick profit.

Continually forcing dogs to mate and produce puppies is incredibly tiring on their bodies, so there are lots of health and welfare complications associated with puppy farms. Not only is this unbearable for the animals, but it often leads to heartache for the new owners who purchase pets with illnesses and complications.

Pair this horrible trend with the fact that beloved pets are being stolen to facilitate this illegal and heinous activity, and it is almost unthinkable. It's an abhorrent business and the thought of it on my doorstep disgusted me. I shared my thoughts with Zola, and she thought I was on the right track.

'My friend has a shih-tzu and told me someone came up to her on the street and asked if she was interested in breeding him and she'd get a cut of the money. She said no, he was neutered anyway, but even so she was outraged,' she told me.

'I guess that's nicer than being stolen, but still very concerning.'

'Yeah, super shady. She hasn't taken him out since, she's way too scared of something like this.' She waved her hand in front of Chestnut, gesturing to the situation she found herself in.

We spoke for a while longer and then I drove her home. She had a flat in a newly built block a short walk from the park. This gave me a flash of inspiration.

'This might seem random, but does your friend with the shih-tzu live in a block or somewhere with a garden?'

'She doesn't have a garden, we often walk our dogs together in the park but she definitely won't now!'

'Interesting . . .' I mumbled, chewing my lip as I often do when I'm mulling things over.

We said goodbye and I said I would let her know if there were any interesting breaks, then I drove home as quick as the speed limit would allow.

I bounded straight into the office, barely greeting Mark, or Alexis, who had popped round for dinner.

Under each pet picture was a bullet list of the key information from each case. After seeing that Zola didn't have a garden, and nor did her friend who was approached on the street, I was able to make another connection.

Before I could report any of this to anyone, I needed to substantiate my claims, so I took this investigation online and hit the dark recesses of the internet to look for sellers in my local area.

It took one search to find a list of unregistered dog breeders in the area. There were countless adverts for breeders selling multiple litters of puppies of various breeds. It wasn't possible to see if these were puppy farms, but it was alarming to see so many adverts just for this area.

I didn't think any of these crimes were opportunistic. I thought they were planned. I just had to figure out what to do about it.

For this specific case, it was becoming increasingly clear that this would be a police investigation. While some of the residents had reported their missing pets, as far as I knew, no investigations had taken place and I seemed to be the only person making a connection between the cases. I hoped that the information I had gathered would have done a chunk of the legwork for the police so that they could hop to it. I had to be very careful that the information I had gathered was as accurate as it could be, and not put myself in a position that could compromise a potential police investigation by providing information that the police couldn't corroborate, or by investigating to the extent that the perpetrators realise they're under scrutiny. With this in mind, I decided this would be the appropriate place for me to stop investigating.

I had all of the details of the suspected puppy farms, and I could easily go to the Kennel Club or other pet charities with this information and let them investigate for themselves. Or I could potentially go undercover and get some video evidence of these so-called businesses; perhaps pretend to be a potential buyer to see if they were legitimate. But, for this particular case, that felt like an overstep. The best course of action for me now would be to report all of my findings and theories to the police, and let them take over.

I started this for the community, who were very concerned about this crime wave. They deserved some sort of resolution, so I picked up the phone and spoke with Terrence from the Neighbourhood Watch, and together we decided I should address the community face to face and share my findings.

DOGNAPPING

I had to wait a month until the next Neighbourhood Watch meeting. It was mid-August now, so some Covid-19 restrictions had been relaxed a bit, but safety was still a top priority. As a nation, we knew a lot more about the virus and face masks were mandated to help stop the spread.

Terrence and Billy opened the meeting to a much larger group than previously. I was suddenly overcome with nerves as they introduced me on to the stage to speak to the gathered community.

'Did you know, in our quiet, sleepy locality, we have a private investigator walking among us?' Terrence announced.

It was such a cringey introduction and I felt embarrassed that he'd chosen those words, as if I was a vampire they'd just discovered masquerading as a resident. There were mumblings throughout the crowd and people whispered, 'Who could it be?'

I wanted to turn and leave; I felt like Terrence was setting them up to be knocked down by little old me. Instead, I walked up the wooden steps on to the stage, feeling like a toddler being marched up there for a preschool pageant.

'Hello everybody,' I began shakily. 'My name is Ali and yes I am, as Terrence says, a private investigator and I've lived in this village for, well, longer than I care to declare!'

The crowd gave a small laugh, which broke some of the tension.

'I'm here today because I have been investigating a

string of pet thefts from a month or so ago. I am pleased to say that, as far as we know, the crime wave is over or has moved on and there have been no more reported thefts in the area. And I'm even more pleased to say that another pet has been reunited with their owner. I got a call last week to say that Bear, Mr Pritchett's prized farm dog, strolled home as if nothing had happened. He was hungry and matted, but is recovering well!' I shot a quick look at Susan – sadly, Frilly was still missing and it looked like she would never be coming back.

'I spent a few weeks gathering lots of information about the case and have reported my findings to the police, who will, hopefully, pick up the investigation, but as of now I haven't been told that they have. I'm here today to talk to you about some of the things the investigation shone a light on, and how you can protect yourselves so this doesn't happen again.'

I looked across the room and could see that I had everyone's full attention. That was in equal parts encouraging and terrifying. I made sure to not look up again if not necessary; instead I focused on the paper I had in front of me, which outlined everything I wanted to say.

'I just want to preface this by explaining that none of this is anyone's fault, apart from the criminals who carried out the act. These crimes were meticulously planned and carried out by an experienced group. This is evidenced by certain factors each case had in common – these were circumstance and breed.

'Every theft, or attempted theft, was of a dog that is a highly sought-after breed.' I didn't dare look at Susan through fear of one or both of us bursting into tears. 'Frilly, for example, was a pedigree dog with a very classic look – and one of the most popular breeds. Bear was a working dog, and a good one at that. There are many more that fit the same criteria, such as Rosie, a former prized breeder. I made the connection when I found out about Chessie, a beautiful cockapoo who was almost taken out of the hands of her owner, Zola, in broad daylight. Only when Zola announced that Chessie was spayed did they back off.'

I heard a few 'I hadn't thought of that' and 'Oh yes she's right's spread across the crowd.

'Secondly, every dog was taken while the owner followed their usual daily routine. This leads me to believe that each dog was watched for some time to establish a pattern to find the easiest time for the snatch. Take Bear, for example – I believe the thieves spent time learning his commands so they could get his attention.'

I looked for Mr Pritchett in the crowd, but he wasn't there. I conjured an image of him sitting happily at home with Bear on his lap and it made me smile.

I carried on explaining my findings and outlined each case as I had on my timeline at home.

'To try to prevent this from happening again, change up your routine, don't "check in" on social media every time you leave your pet at home, avoid tying them up outside shops and, lastly, make sure they are properly identifiable by a collar with your details – but not the dog's name – and a microchip.'

I finished my speech by urging the crowd to use licensed and registered reputable breeders should they wish to buy a pet in the future.

'The best way to stop these criminals is to cut off their income. No demand, no supply needed.'

And with that, the case was closed, and I knew I'd done all I could.

PI Perspective

People often worry about their car being stolen, their house being broken into, their phone being swiped or other 'typical' burglaries.

Investigating a missing pet is vastly different from investigating anything else that has gone missing. There's a level of uncertainty when it comes to missing pets as, unlike possessions, they can wander off on their own. This sort of investigation requires a different approach – it's something like a missing persons' case, but, without the ability to learn about their character to predetermine their moves, it's really tricky to try to navigate. This particular case wasn't a 'missing' case, this was a manhunt.

There were no contracts or plans agreed upon. No client to report back to or hours to log. Just me, with a strong head for investigation and an addiction to finding information.

DOGNAPPING

The lockdowns ended and the country began to heal from the effects of the pandemic, but sadly dognappings haven't gone away. As long as people are willing to buy dogs without following the proper safety protocols, there will be unethical breeders. It's the responsibility of pet lovers to make their horrible business models unsustainable, by always asking to see litters in a home environment with their mothers, and by getting our pets spayed, neutered and microchipped. After all, we're a nation of animal lovers, which makes dognappers a genuine enemy.

Epilogue

First of all, a huge thank you for purchasing my book and I hope that you have enjoyed it. As you have seen, my cases have similar themes, but each one is unique because of the people involved. The end goal is always the quest for truth. With that, it brings with it a complex range of emotions, from betrayal right through to loss. But the one common denominator in all of the cases is that people are more resilient than they think they are. Once we have reached the end of the investigation, in time it often brings peace and with that you can start to heal. My job brings clarity to often quite complex situations. Yet my commitment remains resolute. I will always strive to be the best I can be, and help people who have nowhere else to turn.

Goodbye for now . . .

Acknowledgements

I would like to thank my editor, Ciara Lloyd from Bonnier. I couldn't have asked for anyone better. She got me (which isn't always easy!) and let me be myself.

To my literary agent, Adam Gauntlett from Peters Fraser and Dunlop, for his confidence in me.

To Kelsey Champion, the one person who has been with me all the way through my business, without whom my book would still be languishing somewhere.

To my fellow investigators and support team who have always been there for me with help and advice: Robert Robinson from Sub Rosa Investigations, Timothy Gilman from Cyber Armed Security and also Aaron Barnes-Wilding.

Lastly but definitely by no means least, my family and my fabulous friends. Especially my daughter Alix, who I embarrass on a weekly basis. Thank you all for your love, support and for believing in me.